ANCIENT GREECE? OR FUTURE HOAX . . .

"You think the Emp has some sort of time machine that works inside his force wall, so he can run history over like a film?"

"Something like that."

"Won't work, comrade."

"Why not?"

"The acts we commit in ancient Greece would affect all subsequent history. Therefore, when our own century comes round, we shall never be born as and when we were, so we shan't exist to go back to ancient Greece to commit those acts."

Bulnes refrained from snorting. "I wouldn't jump to conclusions yet. Just because we find a section of Piriefs put back into its Periklean condition, and see a few characters flitting about in bedspreads, we shouldn't conclude that all Greece has been likewise transformed." Bulnes yawned. "In the morning we can go out and ask anybody if he's seen Aristotle."

THE GLORY THAT WAS

L. SPRAGUE DE CAMP

SF
ace books
A Division of Charter Communications Inc.
A GROSSET & DUNLAP COMPANY
360 Park Avenue South
New York, New York 10010

THE GLORY THAT WAS

An ACE Book

Cover art by Steve Hickman

First Ace printing: July 1979

To Isaac Asimov,
who helped to push this one over the hump.

INTRODUCTION

by

Robert A. Heinlein

In the fields of science fiction and of fantasy there are very few humorists. That is not to say that there are not many, many writers in these fields who try to be funny; of the number who try, entirely too many manage to peddle their weary efforts to desperate editors and the depressing results may be found on any newsstand. Most of these attempts are burlesque—and burlesque is an art hard to apply in a field in which there is literally no limit to the imagination; the practitioner is often tempted to use too wide a scoop when a teaspoon would have been more than adequate. An approach almost as common as burlesque is

that of satire, but satire is an even more difficult
steed to ride. To induce a smile, satire must be
subtle; but it has long since been proved that no
satire can be sufficiently broad to be recognized as
such by all readers. There always remains a large,
very vocal, and angry minority who will have
taken the attempted satire with utter seriousness
at its face value and who will thereupon accuse
the author of defaming motherhood, attempting
to cast a smirch on the reader's church and, no
doubt, being opposed to good roads and good
weather.

L. Sprague de Camp is, I believe, the only living
writer in the fields of science fiction and of fantasy whose stories are all (without any exception
that I can remember) consistently humorous.
Other writers in these fields have written truly
funny stories—Henry Kuttner, Theodore Stur-
geon, and Fredric Brown, to give a sample of the
very few who have managed this difficult trick—
but no writer other than de Camp, so far as I know,
has made humor his regular product in science
fiction and fantasy . . . and gotten away with it.

Like standing on one finger, this trick is more
difficult than it looks. Is it possible to analyze how
he does it? Too much literary criticism is dry stuff
at best and too often consists of someone who
can't do the thing he is criticizing nevertheless
explaining to others how the natural artist
achieves his results—and how he should have
done better. The reader is justified in skipping
over the next page or so of this discussion, or,
better yet, skip it entirely and get on to de Camp's
story.

True humor is not cruel, or at least the cruelty is held down to a single dash of bitters. Time was when a rotten egg splashing in the face of the prisoner in the stocks, or a swift kick in the stomach, or even sudden and unexpected death was considered frightfully witty, but our culture has changed and such violence is no longer likely to win a laugh—from most of us. De Camp's humor is never cruel; the pain is bearable, the embarrassment never too sharp. His civilized restraint may lose a few belly laughs (there are few in his stories) but he does not lose his readers through disgusting or dismaying them; instead he takes them along through a long series of warm smiles, contented chuckles, and broad grins. The reader is left with a pleasant glow, a feeling that life is not so bad after all and that the foibles of our monkey race are bearable and even entertaining if one does not take them too seriously.

This, I maintain, is, in an age of hydrogen bombs and iron curtains, a very desirable trick.

The reader is often able to recognize himself in the bumblings and misadventures of de Camp's unheroic heroes and unvillainous villains, and to get there from a rueful but unbitter smile and a feeling of comradeship—and here, I think, lies the principal key to the de Camp brand of humor; he can laugh at himself; he sees himself as just one more of the occasionally noble but always embarrassed race of simian bumpkins, and possibly the most comical of them all. This is the source of the kindness and gentleness of his humor; seeing a man with his foot stuck in a bucket and unable at the moment to shake it off, de Camp will laugh, but with a rueful sympathetic quality which concedes that it may be his turn next to step unexpectedly into a bucket.

It would be easy to go on at length about why I find laughs in de Camp's stories but to do so would be neither entertaining nor instructive. Much of his humor appears to be based on the inappropriate, the out of place, the unexpected, like the classical Horse in the Bathroom. If this does not entertain you, you are not at fault; there are no fixed rules for humor and in the clown business there can be only one immutable law— that which states that the customer is never wrong.

De Camp's stories are always meaty. He brings to his art an astonishing range of knowledge. In addition to formal education and years of experience as an engineer, he knows an amazing amount about an amazingly wide range of subjects—alchemy, aerodynamics, anthropology, archery, ballistics, Barbarossa, Bacchanalia, bimetallism, blastogenesis, cults, cats, catapults, cephalopods, chitons, chlamy—finish the alphabet yourself; you will not be wrong. In fact this man knows almost too much; his erudition would be unbearable were it not so unobtrusive. As it is, he fills his stage with such authentic detail that empathy is built and never broken.

In still another way de Camp preserves empathy with his readers; there is nothing of "Gee-Whiz!" about his stories, no matter how remote or improbable the scene. Even in the Viagens series, although the stage is so large as to require light-speed transportation, the characters are no more than lifesize and the actions are the actions of men, not demigods. De Camp has never destroyed a galaxy and has only rarely and excusably rescued the human race.

This restraint may reduce the flavor for some—but not for me. The best fantasy is usually no more than light wine, the worst mere soda pop, all bubbles and synthetic flavor. The best of the Galaxy Busters are strong Bourbon; the worst are rotgut. In this analogy I would class de Camp's fiction as a very dry Martini.

—R.A.H.

ONE

The *Dagmar II* sank into the trough of the waves, hiding all but her naked poles. As if to take advantage of the momentary shelter afforded by the crests, Knut Bulnes shouted forward, "Any sign of Antikithera?"

"What?" called Wiyem Flin.

"I said, is there any sign of Antikithera?"

Flin shook his head and picked his awkward way aft. When he reached the stern, Bulnes repeated his question.

"No," replied Flin. "But that doesn't mean anything. With this beastly rain on my glasses, I might as well be blind."

"Then go below, if you please, and see if you can pick it up on the scope. It'll soon be too dark for a viz."

Flin hesitated, looking up at the white crest of the nearest wave. He said something that Bulnes could not catch, except for the words "*hippoi Poseidōnos*," then went below.

Bulnes, hoping that Flin would not blow the fuses again, watched his shipmate squeeze his chubby form through the cabin door. Bulnes admitted that it was something to be able to get up from an attack of seasickness that not even the latest antivertigants could cure and spout Classical Greek. On the other hand, Flin was the kind of man who thought that the right to call himself a Greek scholar made up for his other shortcomings.

Lightning flashed in the dusk. Bulnes smiled faintly. A few good ones like that, and the circuit breakers on Antikithera would go. Then, with luck, the *Dagmar II* could slip through before the force wall was re-established. To run into the wall while it was up would not be good for the little yawl and its crew. Nor would it be good to be picked up on the scopes of Antikithera in the act of slipping through the wall into forbidden Greece. Bulnes was gambling on the hope that the personnel of the station would be taking a relaxed view of their duties, just as he had gambled on the chance of a late spring storm.

Flin stuck his head out the cabin door and shouted, "Ten nautical or seventeen metric, on our right."

Bulnes suppressed an impulse to correct the statement to "starboard." Instead, he shouted back, "We'd better edge up to the wall. It's dark enough."

He set their course to azimuth thirty, then turned the rheostat control. The *Dagmar II* quivered and squatted in the water as her bow rose with the added speed. Although darkness and level-blowing rain hid Antikithera, Bulnes could see the aurora-like glow of the force wall ahead. He called down, "Watch out for those rocks!"

Flin shouted something. The pair of islets between Antikithera and her big sister Kithera ought to show up on the oscilloscope in ample time to avoid them—at least with a more competent radar-operator than Wiyem Flin.

A flash of lightning, and the light curtain dimmed for a few seconds. It would take a bigger one than that to knock out the force wall.

Flin came out and shouted, "The rocks are a good four nautical away. Going to run it?"

The light curtain loomed; Bulnes twisted the rheostat control to low speed. The *Dagmar II*, the wind on her port quarter, settled into a long dignified pitch with a little roll at the crest of every buck. As each wave bore her up from behind she slid forward down the slope like a surfboard, then slowed almost to a stop as the crest of the wave passed under her keel and her bowsprit poked skyward on the rear slope.

Bulnes looked speculatively at the great white crests. He didn't like the shaking-up they'd get if they hove to in that position, nor did he like the prospect of turning broadside to the swell in order to circle to kill time. Although it was hard to judge distance in the murk, he guessed the curtain to be no more than a hundred meters ahead.

Then came the granddaddy of all lightning flashes. Thunder roared, and the light curtain blinked out.

"They're out!" yelled Flin. "Why don't you . . ."

Bulnes had already spun the rheostat to "Full." The *Dagmar II* leaped forward, wings of spray rising from her bow. Her pitching ceased as she caught up with the waves and skittered along with them.

Flin said, "I hope we get through before they . . ."

"If you please," interrupted Bulnes, "go below and check the scope again."

Trust Wiyem to put the obvious into words. Of course they hoped the ship would pass through the barrier zone before the electronicians replaced the circuit breakers and the force wall built up again. They ought to be passing through the zone now.

A yelp came from Flin as a misty radiance appeared in the atmosphere around them. Bulnes, gripping his control column, shook as the spasm went through his nervous system. If he once let go, the uncontrolled jerking of his muscles would send him over the side into the black and white smother around them.

Forcing his neck to obey, Bulnes craned it far enough to see that the radiance was mostly astern. If they had been right in the middle of the zone, nothing would have saved them.

The lights went out.

The *Dagmar II* slowed, lost way, and lay drifting before the wind and pitching wildly. Flin's pale round face appeared dimly in the cabin door. "The motor—fuses—stopped . . ."

Bulnes, blessing the caution that had led him to rig the sails against the remote possibility of power failure, felt for the button controlling the flying-jib winch. He pressed it.

Nothing happened.

He shouted to Flin, "Know where the head-lamps are?"

Flin nodded.

"Get a couple, if you don't mind."

The cabin door closed, and the shimmer of the force field faded out astern. Flin reappeared wearing one headlamp and handed the other to Bulnes, who slipped it on over his oilskin hat. The lights cast wan beams into the dark, but with the power off they were the best source of light left.

Bulnes said, "Can you find the crank for the sail winches in the tool locker?"

"I think so."

During Flin's absence Bulnes shifted the steering control from the now useless gyro to the direct-steering wheel. When Flin came out with the crank, Bulnes said, "Kindly take the wheel. Keep the wind on our port quarter."

Bulnes took the crank and worked his way forward. He located the flying-jib winch at the base of the mainmast and inserted the crank. Not having had to hoist sail by hand power for over a year, he hoped the hand winch wouldn't be corroded.

The ship bounced beneath him. He squatted, holding the mast with one hand and the crank with the other, and heaved. The crank moved, sluggishly at first, then faster. The flying jib rose, the light gaskets that held the sail popping, and water spilling out of the folds in the canvas to blow away. The ship began to pick up way as the wind tautened the sail.

When he had hoisted both jibs, Bulnes went aft,

took the wheel from Flin, tested it until he found a stable angle of bearing, and lashed it. Then he and his companion went below.

"I'm soaked," came the plaintive voice of Flin in the dark.

"What d'you expect?" snapped Bulnes. "Get out a flashlight if you please." Flin had made that same remark every time they had run into a blow.

Water sloshed under the floor boards now that the automatic bilge pump had stopped. Bulnes braced himself in the confined space to look at the power plant. With the flashlight added to the beams of the headlamps he soon saw that the case was hopeless. Leads were fused all over the place, and the heart of the system—the great barium-titanite crystal, as big as a small suitcase—had split along a dozen planes of cleavage.

"Surge from the force wall," he grunted. "Raised the interface tensions and broke the crystal all to pieces. We might as well throw this junk overboard."

Bulnes began dismantling the power plant and extracting pieces of the crystal that had powered it. The motor, at least, seemed intact. With a new crystal and some repairs to the wiring, *Dagmar II* would again move under power.

Flin said, "Why didn't you get a spare crystal when we stopped at Marseilles for a recharge?"

Bulnes smoldered. "My dear comrade, where would you store a spare crystal in *here*? Go on forward and hit the sack, if you please. I'll tend to this."

"Really, I must say you don't take these things well. It's not my fault your ruddy crystal broke down."

"Oh, yes? Whose idea was this trip anyway?"

"You should have foreseen . . ."

"I warned you there were risks, my dear sir. And whose wife are we hunting?"

"Mine of course. But don't try to make out that it's all on my account. You were as keen to go as I, in hope of getting a story for your magazine."

"Oh, well," said Bulnes, trying to turn off the acrimony, "I only hope that if we do find Thalia, you'll think she was worth it. Some of my old married friends would be only too glad to have the Emperor's agents kidnap their wives."

"You don't understand these things, Knut. Being a mere selfish bachelor—ouch!"

"Hit your head again?"

"Yes, dash it."

Bulnes smiled. "Where'd you put the booklet of radar instructions? I saw you looking through it today."

"Oh, I don't know—there it is on the floor."

"You mean the deck. Damn it, I wish you'd be so *exceedingly* kind as to put things back where they belong!"

"Sorry. What have you got in mind?"

"To run the radar from the hand-crank generator. It has an attachment, though I've never used it."

Bulnes thumbed through the waterproof instruction booklet by the light of his headlamp. Since a man lacked the strength in his arms to power the transmitting side of the radar circuit, one had to connect up the bank of condensers (C, D, E in Diagram 4) to the output, charge the condensers with the hand crank, switch the hand generator over to the scope circuit, and then close the switch (L in Diagram 6) that discharged the condenser bank through . . .

"Knut," came the voice of Wiyem Flin.

"Yes? I thought you were asleep."

"I'm not sleepy. I was just thinking about wives and marriage and things."

"Well?"

"Look here, old man, why don't you and Dagmar do it? Thalia was telling me Dagmar told her she'd be glad . . ."

"*Caramba!*" shouted Bulnes. "My dear man, my relations with Miss Mekrei are my own damned business! When I want advice on subjects like that, I'll go to a regular psycher. Now kindly shut up and let me work."

"Oh, very well, but you needn't be so blasted touchy."

Still fuming, Bulnes screwed his last connection home. Touchy! Knut Bulnes considered himself, with reason, an even-tempered and self-controlled man, but after two weeks of Wiyem Flin, plus the strain of running the force wall, with God only knew what penalties awaiting him, and on top of that to have Flin offering unsolicited advice about Dagmar . . .

He spun the hand crank. When the generator whined, he flipped the switch. The scope sprang into light, as if a brushful of luminous paint had been swirled against its surface. Bulnes strained his eyes upon the little glass disk to catch every detail before the picture faded. The disk sparkled with sea return, through which he could make out Antikithera well to their rear. There was nothing ahead. As he remembered the charts, there should be nothing in the northeast quadrant within sixty nauticals. By the time they had to look for the Kiklades, it would be day.

Flin's remark still rankled. Hell, Bulnes thought, the world was getting too damned well-organized and everybody in it too well-adjusted and too thoroughly conditioned to make the best of it—at least for an anachronistic individualist like himself, Bulnes thought, smiling a little. He couldn't help a certain sympathy for that fellow in the poem, Miniver Cheevy, who

> ". . . loved the Medici,
> Albeit he had never seen one;
> He would have sinned incessantly
> Could he have been one." *

This new Puritanism was the fault of the last three Emperors. Though denied political power by the World Constitution, they exerted real leadership in manners and morals. Hence while under Kaal IV men became sport fanatics, under Serj III they affected a pallid aestheticism. And whereas under the dissolute Rodri they competed in worldliness, under the strait-laced trio ending with Vasil IX, the incumbent, they . . .

"Knut."

"What now?"

"Sorry, old man. Didn't mean to tread on one of your corns. But I thought you should know—I was about to tell you *that* was why you weren't asked to join the Sphinx Club."

* From *Miniver Cheevy*, by Edwin Arlington Robinson, copr. by Chas. Scribner's Sons.

"So?" said Bulnes in a changed voice. "Interesting. I was just thinking I should have lived in the twenty-first century, when a man's private life was his own affair."

"Oh, I don't think the twenty-first century was so wonderful. For uninhibited freedom, now, take Periklean Athens. Where else could a man walk down the main street stark naked without exciting the least remark?"

"That doesn't prove them unconventional. Nudity happened to be among their conventions, like eating your parents in ancient Ireland."

"A base libel on my Irish ancestors," said Flin. "The Athenians really did pride themselves on letting people do as they pleased so long as they didn't bother other people. Read your Thucydides."

"All very fine for the citizens, but I seem to remember that most of the people of Athens were slaves."

"Still, I'd give anything to see it as it was then."

"Well, my good friend, you'll soon see it as it is now, whatever that may mean. I wonder what Vasil Hohnsol-Romano *has* been up to all these years?"

"That kosker!"

"You surprise me, Wiyem. *Lèse majesté*, no less."

"I mean it. Lenz not only turns Greece over to him for his dashed experiments, but lets him kidnap people's wives because they happen to be Greek. I say!"

"What?" said Bulnes.

"Just remembered something that might have a

bearing on the Emp's activities. I was talking to old Djounz—you know, Maksel Djounz the historian—just before we left England. It seems old Djounz knows a chap named Adler—Ogust Adler—the curator of the Dresden Museum."

"Is he the one who told you your wife had been shipped back to Greece with all the other emigré Greeks?"

"No. That was Dagmar's friend Baiker. Anyway, d'you know those caves or saltmines or whatever they are in Saxony?"

"I've heard of them."

"Some years ago, Djounz says, Adler got orders from His Majesty, down the chain of command, to store some building stone and marble—all carefully crated and numbered. Trainloads of the things, enough to build a city. Took Ogust nearly a year to store them. A couple of the crates broke in handling, and he saw the blocks and says one bore a Classical Greek inscription. It's as if the Emp had dismantled all the ancient ruins in Greece and shipped the pieces to Saxony for storage."

"Very interesting," said Bulnes. "But you'd better get some sleep, if you'll let me say so, because in a few hours I'm going to wake you up to take the con."

TWO

Flin woke him in the gray and spray-clouded dawn, saying, "Could you wrap this around my finger, Knut?"

"What'd you do to it?"

"Burned it on that cooker. I can't seem to make it work."

Bulnes sighed. "God help us if we have to hide from the Emp's men. You'd drop something at a critical moment."

"What'll happen if they do catch us?"

"Then *Trends* will need a new article editor."

"I hope I shall get on with him as well as I have with you." Flin referred to the articles on Roman ruins he had sold Bulnes, which sale had led to their acquaintance.

"Thanks, but you forget that Somerset School will need a new teacher of dead languages, too." He grinned at Flin's stricken expression. "It was

your idea. Now go back on deck, please, while I
get us some coffee."

Bulnes pulled on his shirt and dungaree pants
and splashed water in his face. He squinted at his
face in the glass, noting how the reddish brown
stubble on the cheeks would soon match the
mousquetaire mustache and goatee that both he
and Flin wore. The face combined a swarthy
complexion, a hint of a high-cheeked oriental
look (from his Filipino grandmother), and wavy
hair of an incongruous light brown, receding at
the temples. Altogether Knut Manuel Edger
Bulnes y Nyberg was a pretty mixed type.

A few spins of the generator crank showed
nothing but sea return on the radar scope, and a
look outside revealed only the Mirtoön Sea. Although the wind still drove a drenching spray
across the deck, the rain at least had desisted.

Over breakfast Bulnes said, "Please, remember
our story if we're caught. Our power plant broke
down, and the wind blew us right through the
force wall."

"We might stand on our constitutional rights,"
said Flin.

"What a naïve little man you are!"

"Oh, come now, things aren't really so bad as
that."

"Not in England. Not yet, that is. You ought to
hear some of the stories from the Continent and
from Africa."

"You mean you think Lenz will get around to us
when he's strong enough?"

"Naturally. I suspect Lenz has been giving the
Emp a free hand in Greece to get him out of the

way so he can suppress the Opposition altogether."

"How shocking!" said Flin.

"If you're easily shocked."

"I thought we were all through with that sort of
thing. And the Populists were always strong for
personal liberty."

"That was before they had power. Didn't a
fellow-countryman of yours say something about
'Power corrupts'?"

"I suppose so," said Flin unhappily.

"Constitutional rights will mean something
again when the Populist Party has a real Opposition."

"And where are you going to get that before
Lenz makes himself a world autocrat?"

Bulnes shrugged. "I don't know. I like the program of the Diffusionists, but Wong's a windbag.
Falal Mansur's the ablest Opposition leader, but I
can't imagine voting Asceticist."

"The Populists always had the most en-
lightened program, and they did achieve a lot of
good when they got their majority."

"That," said Bulnes, "is precisely the trouble.
Because they did so much good when they came
to power, they got a large majority; and because
they got such a large majority, they were cor-
rupted by power and are dangerous now. A
paradox, no?"

"If the Emp's brother were alive . . ."

"Probably no better than Vasil. I remember Serj
as a hell-raiser. What did your man Gibbon say
about hereditary monarchy?"

" 'Of all the forms of government devised by

man, it affords the fairest scope for ridicule.' Still, you know what the sociodynamicists said . . ."

As the equinoctal day wore on, the wind moderated enough for Bulnes and Flin to hoist the mizzen sail. Toward dusk the radar showed an island, perhaps four miles long, and shaped something like the Hebrew letter *vau* reversed, a little to starboard of dead ahead. That would be Velvina. Bulnes altered course to pass well to the west of this island into the Saronic Gulf. From time to time he found himself cocking an ear for the ping of the radar alarm that would show him that someone was sweeping the yacht with a search beam—forgetting momentarily that without power, this gadget was dead like all the others.

The wind had now backed to the south, which made tacking unnecessary. It continued to weaken until before dark they hoisted the main as well.

Bulnes, hand-steering the *Dagmar II* by the magnetic compass (the gyrocompass being inoperative), looked at his smart Marconi rig straining in the following wind and thanked his gods that he had put in enough sailing practice to be able to handle her. The ancient skills did come in handy at times, even in this push-button world. Of course with power plant intact he'd have reached Piriefs the previous night.

Still, he should not complain too bitterly. At the present rate they should make the harbor at Athini before morning, and if he could find some Oppositionists ashore, he might even get his power plant fixed.

He lashed his wheel and ducked inside for a look by radar.

"For the love of Ormazd!" he said. "You must *want* attention."

Flin was carefully laying out his city clothes: his best ankle breeches, ruffled shirt, gold-laced jacket, and steeple-crowned hat with plastic plume.

"Well—uh—I wanted to look decent, you know . . ."

"And let me do the dirty work?" Bulnes snorted and addressed himself to the radar. A sweep of the antenna showed the battered triangle of Eyina to port and the double sickle curve of the Attic coast to starboard.

"How's the wind?" asked Flin.

"Still dropping."

They ate. As evening wore on the wind fell to a mere breeze and a fog came up.

Bulnes said, "I think we shall still make Piriefs by morning, but we must take a radar reading every quarter-hour."

"Who'd run us down? Since we ran the barrier we haven't raised a single ship or plane, by viz or radar."

"Now that you mention it, it is queer. Piriefs used to be one of the busiest ports in the Mediterranean. Wonder if the Emp has cleared the area to make a wildlife preserve?"

"Doesn't sound reasonable. What's become of all the Greeks? Why should he send his agents to round up all the Greeks who heard what was coming and fled the country, like my wife's family?"

"Maybe he wants to exterminate them because

of some pseudo-scientific racial theory, like that fellow Hitler in the twen—"

"Gad!" said Flin, eyes popping. "You don't *really* think . . . ?"

"No, not really, old fellow," said Bulnes. "Vasil may have some queer ideas, like being a reincarnation of Henri the Fourth of France and Franklin Roosevelt of the United States, but I've always heard he was an essentially kindly and altruistic soul."

"Kindly and altruistic! When he separates a man from his wife for years . . ." Flin muttered under his breath. "You're no idea how dependent I am on Thalia. If she were gone—well . . ."

"You'd be lost." Bulnes stretched his long arms and yawned. "I'm crawling back into the sack for a couple of hours. Please wake me if we raise another ship or Piriefs on the scope."

It was on Bulnes's watch, however, that the scalloped peninsula of Piriefs came into view on the screen. He let Flin sleep, ducking into the cabin for frequent spins of the generator crank, until Zea Harbor was a mere nautical mile away. Then he awoke him.

Flin blinked behind his glasses. "My goodness, you can't see a thing! Are you going into the harbor in this soup?"

"If we don't raise any ships, I may try it, so long as our short-range tube works."

"Which harbor, the Kantharos? That has the most room."

"Yes, but we should have to work around the west end of the peninsula and through a channel. I don't think that would be smart at night under sail alone. Or we can run before the wind straight into Zea. There should be only small craft there."

As the little yacht crept toward Zea Harbor, pitching slowly on the smooth swells, Bulnes strained his eyes into the dark. He said, "We should see the Fretis Light."

"In this muck?"

"Yes, it's a fog-piercer . . . Take another spin on the crank."

A minute later Flin's voice came out of the cabin: "There seem to be some small ships anchored . . . I should say about thirty meters at the largest. Docks and ship sheds around the edge, too. Bear le— I mean to port."

"Are we through the entrance, please?"

"Just about . . . A little to starboard . . . I see more anchored ships on the screen . . . We must be passing close by one. Don't they show lights?"

"Not a light. Find me a clear space and we'll anchor."

"Righto. Bear to port a point . . . Little more . . ."

"You'll have to drop anchor by hand. Say when, and I'll bring her about. Watch your head if we have to jibe."

After a while, Flin's voice came, "Here you are!"

Bulnes spun the wheel. The *Dagmar II* did a tight turn and luffed, sails flapping gently. Flin bounced out of the cabin and scrambled forward, almost falling over the side. Bulnes could see the diffused light of his headlamp and hear the rattle of the anchor chain. The yacht drifted shoreward until stopped by the anchor. Bulnes and Flin lowered the sails.

"Quietest place I ever saw," said Flin. "We

ought to hear ships loading over in the Kantharos."

Bulnes yawned. "I hear somebody talking on
shore, so the place can't be utterly deserted. Might
as well make ourselves comfortable until morning
. . . Hell, it's not yet midnight."

"Aren't we liable to be run down without
lights?"

"I suppose we are, but I don't know what to do
about it."

"Why can't we take the bulbs out of the sockets
and put candles in their place? That might be
better than nothing."

Bulnes looked with surprise at his partner.
"Splendid! Why didn't I think of that? You take
the port light."

"Why not let me do both, while you take
another look at the screen?"

Bulnes smiled cynically. Anything to get out of
the slave labor of spinning the generator crank!
He went below.

When the screen flashed into light, he saw the
outline of Zea Harbor surrounding them. Though
it looked different from the charts, Knut Bulnes
was still sure he had not entered the Munihia
Harbor by mistake. The light on the screen was
fading when movement caught his attention.

He spun the crank again and threw the switch.

"Hey, Wiyem!" he called, cranking furiously.
The generator whined.

"What is it? I haven't got the starboard . . ."

"Kindly look at this!" Bulnes pointed to the
object, an unmistakable ship moving through the
harbor entrance toward them.

"Looks like a dashed centipede!" said Flin.

"That's the return from the wake. Hurry with that other light, if you please, and if you hear 'em, tell 'em to keep off."

Flin hurried out again. Bulnes took one more spin, then snatched up a flashlight and went out on deck after him. Cocking his ears against the opaque dark, he heard a medley of sounds: a murmur of voices, a ripple of water, and a rhythmic thumping.

He cupped his hands. "Keep off!"

The noise became louder. He shouted again, then said to Flin, "Know where the signal flares are? Get some quick!"

THREE

The sounds grew louder yet. The unseen ship must contain many people all talking at once: an excursion boat, perhaps. Somebody chanted above the general noise: "*Rhyppapai! Papai! Rhyppapai! Papai!*"

The approaching ship must now be so close that her stem might appear any time. In the fog, higher than Bulnes's head, a light spot grew to a hazy red ball.

"Here they are," panted Flin. "I had to hunt . . ."

"Get away! Keep off!" screamed Bulnes in French, Italian, Spanish, and Arabic.

From the darkness a voice answered "*Ti?*" and continued with a rattle of syllables Bulnes could not make out, though it sounded not unlike his native Spanish. The "*Rhyppapai! Papai!*" grew louder, keeping time with the thump and splash as of many oars.

The blood-red ball became brighter. Bulnes snatched up one of the flares and ignited it with his cigarette lighter.

The red ball became a fire pot on the bow of a ship. Bulnes glimpsed a group of men around the fire pot. Then the flare went off, just as something struck the *Dagmar II* under water with a sickening crunch.

The yacht jerked. Bulnes, almost thrown overboard, dropped the flare to clutch for support just as the magenta flame shot out. The flare fell into the water and was quenched with a sizzle. The post or tripod on the strange ship toppled forward, spilling coals over the bow, and the men around it grabbed at each other and at the rail. The *"Rhyppapai!"* stopped.

"You farstards!" howled Bulnes. *"Maricones!"*

Shouts came from the other ship, and water swirled as the ship began to back away.

Bulnes thrust his head into the cabin. By the light of his headlamp he could see that the floor boards were already wet, and an ominous gurgle from below told the rest of the tale. Bulnes snatched up the sail-winch crank and rushed out again.

"Wiyem!" he shouted. "We're filling! Pull up the anchor!"

Bulnes cranked the sail winches furiously, taking the jibs first so that the faint air filled these and swung the yacht's bow shoreward. Water was sloshing over the duckboards by the time they were all up and the ship sliding toward shore.

"She moves awfully slowly," said Flin.

"Not much wind, and she's low in the water."

"My feet are getting wet."

"There'll be more of you wet than that!"

Fuming, Bulnes searched the fog for signs of shore. The water was up to his ankles.

"Did you see what I saw?" said Flin.

"You mean that ship, like some antique out of a history book?"

"More than that. It was a Classical trireme."

"I thought so. Somebody must be making a movie."

"Could be," said Flin dubiously.

"What holed us? The bow of that thing was nowhere near the *Dagmar*."

"If it was a real trireme, it would have a ram sticking out just below the surface of the water."

"What were those people talking? They didn't seem to understand any of the common Mediterranean languages."

"Dashed if I know. Is that something ahead?"

Dark irregularities appeared in the fog forward. The sounds from the galley had sunk to a mere murmur. Bulnes said, "Drop the mainsail. This looks like a wharf."

The water was up to his calves. The wharf solidified, but small ships tied up to it occupied all the available space.

Bulnes said, "She's going down any minute. As soon as we touch those ships, jump on to them."

"But our clothes and stuff . . ."

"Can't be helped. Ready?"

The *Dagmar II* brushed alongside the nearest ship, a blur of curved lines in the blackness.

Bulnes released the wheel and leaped for the rail.
The yacht, as if this latest jar had upset a precari-
ous balance, shuddered and slid below the surface of the bay.

Bulnes swung himself over the rail of the other
ship, then turned as Flin called, "Help me, Knut!
I'm stuck!"

Bulnes found his companion hanging on to the
rail with his hands while his feet thrashed the
water. He hauled the plump schoolteacher over
the rail.

"Ouch!" said Flin. "You needn't be so blasted
rough, you know. Oh, dear, my good clothes and
passport and everything!"

"Clothes! How about my ship?"

"She's insured, isn't she?"

"Yes, but—I loved that little boat."

"Rotten luck, but I should think she could be
raised."

"There is that." Bulnes blew his nose.

"What worries me more . . ." said Flin.

"Yes?"

"This thing we're on is of antique design too.
Just put your hand on these timbers; you can feel
the adze marks. How shall we ever get out of
this—this phantasmagoria?"

"We'll worry about that in the morning, comrade. Come on."

"Where to?"

"To find a place to sleep. Got your money?"

"Yes. That and our clothes and my pocket radio
and your case knife are about our only worldly
goods at the moment."

Bulnes felt his way to the opposite side of the
ship and climbed over the rail to the pier. He

found himself on a flat, stone-paved surface. Ahead, low structures loomed. From somewhere in the ambient darkness, human voices wafted faintly.

Bulnes led Flin a step at a time across the wharf until his groping hand found a wall, then along the wall to a corner. It seemed to be the beginning of a street.

The darkness lay thick ahead. Creeping along this street, they came to another intersection. A ruddiness in the fog to the right suggested a fire, and voices came from that direction.

"Shall we try 'em?" said Bulnes.

"I don't know. I suppose we might as well. If I could only get dry for once!"

They walked toward the light, and the ruddiness solidified into a red globe, like a planetary nebula contracting into a star. The red ball in turn became a wood fire crackling in an iron cage atop a stone pillar in the middle of a street crossing.

Bulnes saw four men squatting or kneeling in a circle, looking inward at the ground, while two others stood behind them watching. At the sound of footsteps, they looked around. All had beards. All were clad in shapeless pieces of cloth wrapped around their persons. Bare arms and legs protruded from these bundles. They stank of garlic, onions, olive oil, and unwashed human hide.

As the nearest man, who had had his back to them, swiveled around on his heels Bulnes saw a little group of white objects on the ground. He had interrupted a crap game.

"Pu ime?" he said in Greek, of which he knew a few phrases.

The men looked at one another. One made an

unintelligible remark. Although the language sounded European, it had a curious singsong quality.

Bulnes repeated his question.

Again the interchange of unknown syllables, and a laugh. Six pairs of eyes focused on Bulnes.

Beside him, Flin burst out, "Knut! I'll swear they're talking *Classical Greek!*"

"*Caray!* Suppose you take over, then."

"I don't know . . . I'll try, but we don't learn to use the stuff colloquially in school, you know." Flin addressed the men, "*Chaire.*"

All the men were now up. The nearest was shorter than the others but very broad of chest and thick of biceps.

"*Chaire,*" repeated this one, his pitch sliding up and down on the first syllable.

"*Pos echeis?*" said Flin.

"*Agathon,*" grinned the stocky man. More remarks flew among the six. Bulnes asked, "What are they saying?"

"Can't quite make out, but I jolly well don't like it. I'll ask the way to an inn." Flin began piecing together a sentence, a word at a time.

Bulnes saw one of the men pick up a club he had left lying on the ground. This was going to be like that time in Bombay. He glanced at the sheath knife at his own waist. When Flin had finished his sentence, Bulnes murmured, "Got a knife in your pocket?"

"Y-yes, but . . ."

"Get your hand on it, please. If they jump us, try to get your back to the pillar."

Bulnes and Flin stood about as far from the

pillar as the strange sextet, who had been playing their game at some distance from its base because the fire did not illuminate the ground directly below itself. Flin started his sentence again, but the six seemed not to be paying attention. Instead they leaned toward the stocky one, listening to the words he muttered.

Bulnes quietly unsnapped the retaining loop that held the upper end of his knife handle, then started to peel off his greasy work jacket. He had it partly off when the burly man said something that sounded as if it began with "happy teeth."

At the same time that man's fist came out of his swathings with a knife.

FOUR

As the six, spreading out into a crescent with the horns forward, advanced with knives and cudgels, Wiyem Flin uttered a mouselike noise and ducked behind Knut Bulnes.

Bulnes, instead of backing, took a step forward and aimed a terrific kick at the crotch of the stocky leader. Though the kick flew a little short, the rope-soled espadrille sank into the paunch of the fellow. As Bulnes recovered, the stout man fell to his hands and knees with a feral grunt.

By this time Bulnes had his jacket off, coiled around his left forearm, his case knife in his other hand. As one of the men stepped forward, bringing down a knife-bearing fist in an overhand stab, Bulnes caught the point of the knife in the jacket. With an underhand outward thrust he stabbed the man in the solar plexus. The man screamed and fell.

Then Bulnes had his back to the pillar, his eyes flicking from man to man. He was dimly aware of Wiyem Flin beside him, making feints with a pocket knife.

Now that two of their comrades were down, the four remaining attackers seemed to have lost their *elan*. They danced in and out, arms upraised for a stab or a blow, crying: "*Epitithete! Sphazete autous!*" but not closing.

Bulnes caught another blow on his rolled-up jacket. Although his left arm was beginning to feel sore, each time they came in he drove them back with feints and thrusts. His task was lightened by the fact that these *ladrones* seemed not to know any way of using a dagger except the easily blocked overhand stab. The stout man Bulnes had kicked was not getting up.

A sound beside him drew the attention of Bulnes in time to see Wiyem Flin, having taken a cudgel blow on the pate, slide limply to the ground. Now Bulnes knew there was no chance for him. One man, be he ever so agile, cannot face in three directions at once . . .

Another sound transpierced the foggy night: a *whish* of cloven air concluded by the sharp report of wood striking a human cranium. The burly man whom Bulnes had kicked in the belly staggered forward, plowing through the semicircle of his own people with head down as if to butt Bulnes in the midriff.

As the man came near, Bulnes brought his fist up in an underhand jab, sinking his knife blade into the fellow's throat. At the same time the noise from beyond the circle was heard again: *whsht-*

thuck! whsht-thuck!, together with a hoarse yell.

The stoutish man collapsed across the inert Flin, while Bulnes sighted another figure leaping about behind his assailants, beating them over their heads with a stick or staff, and shouting. The remaining attackers turned in confusion to see who was taking them in the rear. Then the whole lot were gone.

As his rescuer came forward into the firelight, Bulnes saw a stocky, bearded man wearing what first looked like an outfit of modern working clothes. However, the firelight soon showed profound differences: trousers tucked into soft-leather boots; a jacket of coarse material whose hem dipped to a low point in front and which was held closed by a wide belt, without benefit of buttons. And on his head he wore a kind of gnomish felt helmet or cap that covered his ears and rose to a tall point, his long hair escaping from under its lower edge. The general effect was that of somebody dressed up to play a medieval Russian peasant in *Prince Igor*. His weapon was an unstrung bow, and from his belt a quiverful of arrows hung over one hip.

"*Chaire!*" said the newcomer, and followed the salutation with a string of gibberish.

Bulnes shook his head and replied: "Thanks, but who are you?"

More unintelligible sounds.

"Is this"—Bulnes waved an arm—"Piriefs?"

Light dawned on the stranger's face. "*Esti ho Peiraieus!*" he said, and then went off into another spate of chatter.

Bulnes turned to succor Flin, whose balding

head was rising out of the cone of darkness around the base of the pillar.

Flin's uncertain voice came "*Ei Skythotoxotes?*"

"*Pany men oun,*" replied the man. He and Flin spoke, the former swiftly, Flin more slowly. After several interchanges Flin turned to Bulnes.

"He's a copper. One of the corps of so-called Scythian archers, slave-policemen owned by the city of Athens in ancient times. Where the deuce are my glasses?"

"How'd he happen to be here so opportunely?"

"His present duty is that of night guard in the Arsenal of Philon, and he heard the racket. He wants to know what part of Greece you come from—says you have the strangest accent he ever heard."

"No use telling him I'm from three thousand years in the future. Is that really Classical Greek you're chattering?"

"Absolutely," Flin said. "Though he seems to have a terrific accent himself. Natural, if he's a Scythian or Thracian."

"So to talk to him in modern Greek is like using modern English on King Alfred?"

"Exactly so. Ah, here they are!" Flin had found his glasses.

The archer spoke.

"What's that?" asked Bulnes.

Flin explained, "He says we shall have to come with him to the office of his superior here in the Peiraieus."

"What then?"

After further dialogue Flin continued: "We

shall be held there for the rest of the night, and tomorrow we shall be taken up to Athens for a hearing before the Polemarchos."

"Who's he?"

"He presides over criminal cases involving foreigners."

Bulnes said, "Whatever weird sort of business is going on, I don't care to be caught up in the official gears. Ask him who these stiffs are, if you please."

"He says the fat one is a notorious local gangster, a lieutenant of someone called Phaleas."

"Then even he should be able to see we're guilty of no crime. Why can't we bribe him to help us drop the corpses in the harbor and let us go?"

"What, bribe an official in the performance of his duty?"

"Oh, come off it, my dear Wiyem. This isn't England. It's either ancient Greece or a good facsimile thereof."

"But—but . . ."

"If this lad's a slave, they probably don't pay him anything, so he's used to grafting a bit in order to enjoy some of the comforts of life. Go ahead, ask him."

Flin put his question and reported, "He won't say yes or no. It depends on the amount, I suspect."

"What's the purchasing power of our coins?"

"Rather high. One should be able to live comfortably for a month on a modern half-kraun."

Bulnes dug into the change-pocket of his dungarees and examined his coins by the firelight. One silver half-kraun; four silver franks; one silver daim; three aluminum five-pens; five copper pens, and a copper half-pen. A complete assortment of the Empire's coinage—if you did not count the big silver krauns used in some parts of the world in lieu of their paper equivalent.

He handed Flin a frank and said, "Try this."

There followed a lengthy palaver. At last the archer grinned and popped the coin into his mouth. Flin said, "I explained it's a Tartessian drachme. We're Tartessians."

"What are Tartessians, if you please?"

"And you a Spaniard! Tartessos was a famous ancient city that once flourished near Cadiz. Since the Tartessians were considered a rich and civilized people, I thought passing ourselves off as such would give us the most prestige."

The archer leaned his bow stave against the pillar, knelt, and began to strip the bodies.

"What's he doing?" asked Bulnes.

"He says that, confidentially, he sells their clothes and effects. If we don't tell on him, he won't tell on us."

"What does he expect to get for them?"

"Since they were rather well worn to begin with, and now have got knife holes and bloodstains, he doubts he can get a couple of oboloi apiece."

"How much was an obolos?"

"About two pens. There are a couple."

The archer had thrust a finger into the mouth of one of the corpses and dug out a couple of plump little coins about as big around as a pencil. After a similar investigation of the other cadaver he stood up, and grasped the ankle of the gang leader's corpse. He spoke.

Flin said, "He wants us to help him drag these bodies to the waterfront!"

"What's wrong with that? Take the other end of the big stiff, and I'll manage the little one myself."

"*Touch* them? I—I can't!" bleated Flin.

"*Su madre!*" roared Bulnes, then got control of himself. "My dear old man, please pull yourself together, unless you want to get your fool throat cut. . . . Grasp his ankle firmly. There now, it doesn't hurt!"

They set off, dragging the bodies through the mud. Bulnes said, "He agrees we're at Piriefs, but we might try to find out *when*."

"I'll ask . . . He says it's the archonship of Apseudes."

"When was that? Or perhaps I should say, when is it?"

"Blessed if I know."

"I thought you knew all those things."

"Be reasonable, Knut. Could you give the names and dates of all the Spanish kings from Euric on down?"

"I see. Either we've gone back in time, the way they do in those fanciful stories, or somebody's staging a colossal hoax. You might ask him about places to sleep."

"He says there's an inn, but it's full of bedbugs."

"Hm. And I suppose we shall be either swindled by the innkeeper or murdered by another gang of cutthroats . . ."

They came to a pavement ending in a sea wall, beyond which Bulnes saw the glimmer of water.

"*Ballete!*" said the archer. Bulnes heaved on his corpse, and the body splashed into the water. The other followed.

Bulnes thought fast. Unless prevented, the archer would now amble off into the night, leaving him and Flin to start their hunt for shelter all over again. He said, "Let's walk him back to his arsenal. What's his name?"

"Triballos. I've told him you're Bouleus and I'm Philon."

"Why?"

"No Greek would bother pronouncing a foreign name, so we might as well use the nearest Greek equivalents."

Flin resumed his halting conversation with Triballos while Bulnes stalked behind them, deep in thought. The Scythian would have to be used with care. On one hand, the man was a link to this strange world they had blundered into. On the other, Triballos, though technically a slave, was an official; and something told Bulnes that contact with officials was to be avoided by a pair of illegal visitors.

Another formless, fiery glow appeared in the fog. As Bulnes came closer, he saw it was made by a torch in a wall bracket on the front of a large building.

Bulnes fished out his daim and handed it to Flin, saying, "Kindly tell him we'll give him this for those costumes and a lodging for the night in his arsenal."

"What d'you want with those rags?"

"You'll see. Tell him, please."

When the offer had been translated, the archer looked at the coin, weighed it in his palm, and finally broke into a grin.

"He says all right," explained Flin.

The Scyth pushed open one of the two big

doors, took the torch from its bracket, and led the travelers inside. The building proved long and relatively narrow. They stood at one end of a central nave bounded by two rows of pillars. A stone balustrade connected the pillars of each row, with a bronze latticework gate in each intercolumnation. On the sides of the building Bulnes could see the spidery shapes of frames on which sails were stretched, and piles of spars, oars, and timbers.

"*Entauthoi!*" said the archer, leaning his bow against the balustrade. He opened one of the gates and led the visitors to a stair to the gallery overhead. Here the flicker of the torch showed shelves along the outer wall of the building (interrupted at intervals by windows) on which were piled coils of rope. Thicker hawsers were coiled on the floor. Triballos spoke.

"He says," said Flin, "we can sleep on the rope, but we shall have to be up and out before dawn so as not to get him into trouble."

Bulnes watched as the torch receded down the stairs, throwing back distorted shadows. "What's your opinion?"

"About what? Gad, my head aches!"

"About this alleged ancient Greece? Have we slipped back in time, or is it all an act? Or are we dreaming or dead?"

"I think we're really back in ancient Attika."

"Why, my dear sir?"

"The little details."

"You think the Emp has some sort of time machine that works inside his force wall, so he can run history over like a film?"

"Something like that."

"Won't work, comrade."

"Why not?" said Flin.

"The acts we commit in the ancient Greece would affect all subsequent history. Therefore, when our own century comes around, we shall never be born as and when we were, so we shan't exist to go back to ancient Greece to commit those acts."

"We haven't affected history yet."

"We've killed two men, fought four others, and bribed still another."

"But they're not persons of importance!"

"Still, I can imagine the effect of these acts spreading out like ripples until they affect all history. Besides, the *Dagmar*'s lying on the bottom of Zea Harbor. If they dragged her ashore, she'd give them some neat ideas on shipbuilding. With a Marconi rig and a magnetic compass they could discover the Americas a couple of thousand years before anyone did. That would change history all right!"

Flin said, "Well then, if we'd affected history, we should have vanished like a puff of smoke, I suppose. And since we haven't vanished, it's evident your paradox won't hold water."

"If you assume that this *is* ancient Attika. I should say it is evident, rather, that we aren't back in time. By the way, have you any more exact idea of when we are? 'Ancient Greece' covers a lot of centuries."

"Mmm," said Flin. "While I don't know when Apseudes was archon, I think this ruddy building was built late fifth century B.C. Therefore we can't be earlier than that."

"When does that put us? The Persian invasions?"

"No, later. The age of Perikles and the Peloponnesian War—the Golden Age of Greece. It's the real thing, too."

"What makes you so sure?"

"Call it intuition."

Bulnes refrained from snorting. "I wouldn't jump to conclusions yet. Just because we find a section of Piriefs put back into its Periklean condition, and see a few characters flitting about in bedspreads, we shouldn't conclude that all Greece has been likewise transformed." Bulnes yawned. "In the morning we can go out and ask anybody if he's seen Aristotle."

"But Aristotle wouldn't be born yet . . ."

"And if we find him, we'll pinch him to see if he's the real Aristotle or only some ex-restaurateur in a tablecloth and three safety pins."

"All joking aside . . ."

"Please, comrade! If you insist on talking, I shall become wide awake again and get no sleep tonight. Good night."

FIVE

Several factors conspired to awaken Knut Bulnes well before the sunrise of which Triballos had warned him: the song of the birds, the sound of voices without, the snores of Wiyem Flin, and the unyielding nature of the pile of rope that Bulnes had made his bed. There were also his own inner turmoil and excitement. What the hell had they stumbled into? Could they ever hope to get back?

Bulnes sat up, rubbing his itchy eyes. Flin still lay asleep, a large lump showing in the predawn light through the sparse hair that thinly veiled his pink scalp.

Bulnes went to the nearest window: a simple rectangular hole provided with a crude wooden shutter, now wide open. As he stuck his head out the window the sound of high voices came more loudly, though he could not see the source of the sound. The immediate neighborhood seemed to

be filled with buildings not at all like gracefully
columnated Greek temples: crudely plain one-
storey brick structures without outside windows
or decorations.

The owners of two of the voices came in sight: a
pair of young women in long-draped coverings,
each balancing a large jar on her shoulder. Slave
girls fetching the day's household water from the
nearest public fountain, thought Bulnes. If a fake,
it was a most convincing one.

Though absorbed in this spectacle, Bulnes became aware of a melancholy within him which he
finally identified as sorrow for the loss of his
yacht. He braced himself with the thought that if
he ever got out of this, he'd have the most remarkable piece *Trends* had ever published. That is, if
Prime Minister Lenz had not assumed autocratic
power and imposed a censorship.

As the girls passed out of sight, a man hurried in
the other direction, bearing a bundle upon his
shoulder. In the quarter-hour that followed,
others appeared. Bulnes watched, fascinated,
until the waxing light warned him that he would
do well to waken Flin.

Flin, shaken, muttered: "Nex' watch already?
Where are my oilskins— Oh, goodness gracious,
then it wasn't just a bad dream of being back in
ancient Greece!"

He bounced up from his coil of rope and hurried
to the window. Bulnes remarked, "You've been
talking about how you'd love to step back into
ancient Attika, my dear Wiyem, so now's your
chance. I fear, however, we shall be conspicuous
in dungarees and yachting caps."

"You mean to wear those?" Flin indicated the

heap of native garments salvaged from the casualties of the night before.

Bulnes grinned at his companion's expression of distaste. "Yes. How the devil d'you put 'em on?"

"We'd better look them over for—ah—parasites first."

They dragged the garments to the window, shook them, and began inspecting. Bulnes said, "Hell, this thing's nothing but a big rectangle of cloth. No sleeves, no tailoring at all!"

"Of course. That's a Doric chiton. Ah, got one!"

"Good for you. How d'you wear it?"

"Fold it so and wrap it around you under the armpits. These safety pins will fasten it together over both shoulders and along the open side. If you'll take off your clothes, I'll drape you."

"I feel like the model of some damned couturier," said Bulnes. "Ouch!"

"Sorry, didn't mean to prick you. There!"

Bulnes took a few experimental steps. "Draftiest damned thing I ever wore. Now it's your turn, dear comrade . . . What are the remaining pieces? The big ones?"

"Himatia or cloaks. You drape one around yourself any way you like."

"What keeps it in place?"

"A *kalos k'agathos* holds it with one hand. That's how you know he's a gentleman—his hands aren't otherwise occupied."

Bulnes experimented with the blanket-like rectangle of cloth. "Shouldn't there be belts to go around these chemises?"

"I don't see any. Perhaps they got lost in the dark."

"Then we'll steal a little of the Athenian navy's cordage," said Bulnes, making for a pile of light rope with his knife.

"What about our things?"

"You can stuff your watch and pocket knife into your wallet and hang your wallet over your belt, I suppose. Our own clothes we shall have to wad up and hide here."

Flin looked out the window. "I say, the fog's gone and the sun'll be up any minute."

"We shall have to go then." Bulnes tried on the larger of the two pairs of sandals that had belonged to the dead men.

"And start hunting for Thalia?"

"Not so fast! We don't even know she's here yet. We want to know just what we've gotten into first. Also, we shall have to secure a supply of meals, and you'll have to teach me enough Classical Greek to get along on."

"That shouldn't be hard, since you know Romaic." Flin rested his chin in his hand, then snatched away the hand. "We can't even shave—though this seems to be one of the bearded periods. At that we shall be conspicuous in these whiskers." He stroked his mustache and goatee.

"A few more shaveless days will fix that. Where can we get our money changed?"

"There was a building here called the Deigma, where the bankers had tables. They'll probably try to swindle us."

"When would they be open for business?"

"Around dawn. Nearly everything starts at that time."

Bulnes shuddered. "We seem to have fallen among people who take the old saying about early to bed seriously."

"Naturally, in the absence of an advanced lighting system."

Bulnes grimaced. "One word, Wiyem. When you don't like anything, please don't say loudly: 'This is outrageous—we'd never stand for it in Britain!' "

The streets were filling fast, not only with men in the garb of ancient Greece, but also with others: a few Negroes, some swarthy, shaven men whom Flin identified as Egyptians, bearded ones in jerseys and kilts who he said were Phoenicians, and various others. From time to time Bulnes and Flin were forced to dodge a burden beast, a cart, or the contents of a slop pail.

They climbed partway up the hill of the Munihia (or Mounychia, as Flin called it) near the arsenal, until their street petered out. Thence they saw the checkerboard plan of the Peiraieus stretching off to the southwest. In the other direction the Long Walls extended several miles inland toward Athens proper. The sun was just rising over the oak-clad swell of Mount Hymettos. As the sunlight compassed Mount Aigaleos to the north and crept eastward across the valley, something gleamed over Athens.

Flin burst out, "It's the helmet of the Athene of Pheidias—the so-called Athene Promachos—on the Akropolis! They said you could see it from here. This *must* be real!"

"What's that, a statue?"

"A big one, ten meters tall. This is simply wonderful!"

"Some food would be even more so," said Bulnes.

When Flin had feasted his eyes, they walked back down the hill toward the Kantharos Harbor, passing an open space in which stood a number of statues and other monuments, among which hucksters shouted their wares. The thickening crowd was almost entirely male. Nobody paid Bulnes and Flin any attention. Flin asked a man the way to the Deigma.

"What did he say?" asked Bulnes.

"He's a stranger here himself."

The next inquiry brought a more cogent response, and soon they found the Deigma: a huge covered colonnade full of noisy humanity. The garlic stench was almost overpowering.

One section of the Deigma was devoted to banks. Each bank comprised a large table at which sat the banker, surrounded by his slaves, his cash boxes, and his rolls of papyrus accounts. In front of most of these tables a group of customers had lined up.

"How much change have you?" inquired Bulnes.

Flin counted. "Three franks, four daims, one five-pen, six pens, three half-pens."

"Take a frank and try three or four of these fellows to see who'll give us the best price."

"Dash it all, I hate haggling," grumbled Flin, but lined up before the first banker's table.

By the time he had reached the third lineup, Flin was complaining about his feet. Even Bulnes admitted feeling a little faint from hunger and from the waves of garlic odor.

"Just this once, and we'll decide which to deal with . . ."

"Hey!" said a third voice in English, "Are you the guys who showed up in the Peiraieus last night in civilized clothes and was attacked by Phaleas' gang?"

Bulnes and Flin turned. There stood a muscular young man with a round, snub-nosed, innocent-looking face, clad like their rescuer of the previous night in coat, pants, and pointed cap, and leaning on the bow of a Scythian archer.

SIX

"Yes, said Bulnes. "Who are you, if I may ask?"

The youth advanced with hand outstretched. "My name's Diksen, Roi Diksen, from Yonkers. The Gricks calls me Pardokas."

Bulnes and Flin identified themselves, the latter adding, "What are Yonkers?"

"A town in the U.S.A. You guys English?"

Bulnes said, "Flin is. I am by adoption only."

"Where'd you come from originally, huh?"

"I'm technically Spanish, though by descent I'm a little of everything."

"You talk kind of like an American."

"I went to school there. How'd you hear about us?"

"Triballos told me, so I came down from Athens to find you. Been hunting all over the Peiraieus."

"How'd you get off from duty?"

"This is my off-time. I'm on night patrol work.

What you two up to? Changing your dough into this Grick stuff?"

"Yes," said Bulnes.

"How much they giving you?"

"The last banker there said he'd let us have half an obolos for one pen. How does that sound?"

"Pretty fair. I dunno how you done it—these Gricks is full of tricks. But say, when you get done, ain't there some place we can talk?"

"How about a place to eat? We haven't had breakfast, and it must be nearly noon."

The young man's face took on a look of disgust. "A-a-agh, these Gricks don't know nothing about real breakfast. They stick a hunk of bread in their lousy wine and call that a meal. What wouldn't I give for a good old plate of ham and eggs . . . But you guys want lunch. Okay, I know a joint."

Flin had reached the head of his line. Since this banker offered a rate of exchange a shade over those of the preceding two, Flin and Bulnes disposed of all their silver and copper. The aluminum coins, Bulnes knew, they were stuck with.

"Lead on," said Bulnes to Roi Diksen.

The "Scythian" conducted them out of the Deigma. The spring day had turned clear and cloudless. Diksen stopped at the Agora and directed his companions to buy what they wanted for lunch.

". . . on account of these joints'll cook grub for you but they don't carry it themselves—you gotta bring it with you. Ain't that a hell of a way to run a business?"

They turned in at an inn where they sat on

benches facing each other across an elongated table.

"At least," said Bulnes, "it only stinks to low heaven here."

The meal that Diksen had assembled comprised a huge piece of bread, onions swimming in oil, and wine. Bulnes tasted the wine. "Phew!" he said. "Essence of pine cones!"

"You get used to it," said Diksen, "like you get used to the way they soak everything in olive oil. O Kallingos!" He spoke to the proprietor in broken Greek and handed him the onions.

Bulnes said, "Now, Mr. Diksen, what's your story?"

"Well, it's like this, see? I save up the dough I get working for Kaplen's Hardware Store in Yonkers so I can take me a trip to Europe on my vacation. My girl thinks I need Culture. Of all the . . . Anyway, everything goes fine till I get to Beograd. I'm walking through that big cathedral with the other trippers listening to the guide spout ancient history when everything goes black and I wake up at sea."

"What sea?" asked Bulnes.

"Dunno exactly—somewheres north of here. I'm in this boat with chains on my wrists and ankles, see, and a lot of other poor devils with me. We're in a kind of a pen at the bow, and the rest of the ship's full of guys pulling on long oars. I ask the nearest one what gives, but we don't understand each other's languages. These Gricks is all pretty ignorant—there ain't a one of 'em speaks English.

"At night the sailors steer the boat into shore

and run the bow on the beach so they can get out
to stretch and sleep, but they leave us in the boat
with a couple of guys with spears to see we don't
try nothing. After a coupla days we come to the
Peiraieus. I'm all the time waiting to wake up from
this horrible dream, but I don't. They take us to a
place where they sell slaves—nobody told me but
I figured it out. They take off our clothes and make
us stand on the block like in the movies while
guys bid for us.

"When my turn comes I stand up feeling kinda
funny on account of there's a coupla broads
watching, but these Gricks is all nudists, see, and
don't make no never-mind. The auctioneer pokes
me and hollers to look see how strong I am. He
even raps me on the silver plate I got in my head
on account of I was in an automobile accident a
coupla years ago. I don't like it, but there's a big
mean-looking guy with a whip just in case.

"By and by a jerk comes up and talks to the
auctioneer and then asks me something. I don't
get it, so he does sign language of shooting a bow
and arrow. I never shot no bows and arrows since I
was six, so I shake my head. But since that means
'yes' among the Gricks, the jerk thinks I can shoot.
So he goes into a huddle with the auctioneer, and
next I know me and two other guys is being
marched all the way to the police barracks in
Athens.

"When I get onto the language a little, I find out
the jerk is a police commissioner sent down to buy
three new cops for the force. Good thing he
thought I said 'yes' because if he hadn't, I'd either
been sent to the silver mines at Laureion and

worked to death, or sold to a private buyer as a household slave—and what happens to them, I'd just as soon be dead.

"The first days is rugged, on account of the old-timers put us through the jumps. I make like I don't mind on account of I know if I blow my top and slug one of these farstards, they'll beat me to a bloody pulp. All the time I'm trying to pick up a little Grick. And I figure I better learn to shoot quick or it's the silver mines for me. So I watch the boys practicing on the archery range, and when everybody that ain't on duty is asleep after lunch, I sneak out and shoot some. Got my knuckles skinned at first, but at least I don't look like I never touched one of the things before.

"Since then I been trained and put on regular patrol duty like any other cop. As slavery, it ain't too bad. So that's my story. I musta been here nearly a year now. What's yours, gents?"

Bulnes told their story, ending, "We're delighted to make your acquaintance, Mr. Diksen, but we should still like to know a few things. How did you know us by sight?"

"The whiskers. Either you better cut 'em off or stay out of sight for a week until the rest of your hair grows out, see?"

"Otherwise?"

"You mean what would happen? I dunno, but there's something funny about this whole setup."

"The prize understatement of the year. Go on."

"I mean, what is this? It looks like we been dumped back in one of those ancient times they used to tell us about in school. What I wanna know is, what's the deal? The gimmick? They can't really put us back in some other time. It ain't logical."

"Precisely what we've been trying to figure out," said Bulnes. "Do you know of any other cases like ours?"

"Well, one of the boys on the force was telling about another guy, a few months ago, who showed up in modern clothes. I didn't see him myself, but they say he got sent to Laureion."

Bulnes finished his last onion. At least, now, he'd stink like all the others.

"What do we do next?" he asked.

"Well, us modern men got to stick together, see? I thought maybe I'd get next to some guy who knows what it's all about. And how can we get the hell out of here?"

"Why?" said Flin. "Don't you like it?"

Diksen gave a sharp howl that made the other customers look around. "Like it! My God, you just try being a slave and see how you like it!"

"But as a slave you have rather a good position. Athenian slaves were treated the most leniently of any . . ."

"I still got to do like I'm told. If the job was twice as good, I still wouldn't like it, on account I can't quit."

"Suppose you were a free man. Would you like Athens then?"

"Hell no!" said Diksen. "You can keep your pretty statues. I'll take flush toilets and glass windows and electric lights. There ain't nothing in this whole place we'd call necessary for human comfort—even in the rich citizens' houses. Living here's like—like camping out without no modern camping equipment, see? Give me good old Yonkers! Look, professor, you gotta get me back! You gotta, before I go nuts!"

Bulnes said, "We'll try. We, too, have been wondering whether this was the real ancient Greece or a modern imitation."

"How can you tell?" said Diksen. "I never studied no history, so I dunno if it's the McCoy or not."

"For one thing, assuming time travel is really involved, we don't know whether we're back in the whole ancient world or only a part of it."

"Come again, Mr. Bulnes?"

"How shall I explain it? Suppose we started walking north from here. We should pass through Boiotia and Thessalia and so on. Now, in the modern world, there's a force wall around Greece and adjacent areas which the Emp set up to keep people out while he performed his experiments. Do you follow me so far?"

"Yeah, I guess so."

"Well then, in walking away from here, should we eventually come to the force wall again—the same one we penetrated on our way in—or should we just find more and more of the ancient world no matter how far we went?"

Diksen scratched his head. "I dunno. I couldn't start on no hike like that, on account of the epheboi watch the borders to see no runaway slave don't sneak through."

Flin asked, "How about a free man, or somebody who could pass as one?"

"I suppose he could get through, except they tell me it's rough out in the sticks. Bandits and

lions, and if you can't take care of yourself, nobody else ain't gonna do it for you."

Bulnes asked. "D'you know how far this piece
of the ancient world does extend?"

"Lemme think. Most of us archers comes from
what would be the Balkans. They was all farmers
or sheepherders living in little one-room shacks,
and none of 'em ever heard of the World Empire or
longevity treatments or rockets to Mars. No, I
don't think Bulgaria and Romania is inside the
force wall, on account of my ticket took me to
Sofia and Bucuresti. So we must be back in the
real ancient world, two-three thousand years before we was born."

"Not necessarily. This experiment has been
going on for less than a dozen years, yet we see
middle-aged and elderly men all around us, all
convinced they're authentic Athenians."

"How do you méan?" asked Flin.

"If there's some system of introducing a false
memory into a man's mind, so he thinks he's
spent the fifty years of his life in ancient Athens,
the same treatment could be given Mr. Diksen's
fellow-archers, regardless of where they actually
came from. Is there a real Sparta too, Mr. Diksen?"

"Must be," said Diksen. "Coupla months ago
they ordered us out on special duty because a
gang of ambassadors came from there to dicker
over some treaty with the big shot. Bunch of sour-
pusses with long hair, and even dirtier than the
Athenians, which is pretty dirty, see? Well, the
Athenians ain't got no use for Spartans on account
of they got no brains, no manners, and no art, so
the big shot ordered us to escort these ambas-

sadors in case some wise guy heaves something at them. But everything went off okay and the big shot got his treaty."

"Who," asked Bulnes, "is the big shot?"

"The boss—the general—the head strategos. Perikles."

"Oho!" said Flin. "Now we're getting our period narrowed down. There isn't any war with Sparta right now?"

"No. There was some talk about it, but that died down."

"Then we must be before the Peloponnesian War. How old does Perikles look?"

"Hard to say, on account of people got old so much faster in the old days. If he was a modern man, I'd say he was around a hundred or a hundred and ten, but if he's a real ancient Grick, I say sixty maybe."

"When does that date us, Wiyem?" asked Bulnes.

"In the 430's—perhaps as close as 435 to 432 B.C. The Peloponnesian War should be just about to break out. Wish I could remember the details of the opening of the war."

Diksen gulped. "You mean we got a war on our hands, too?"

"If history follows the same course it did the first time. That was the war that ruined Classical Greece. If I'd known what I was getting into, I'd have brought a copy of Thucydides."

"How ja know this ain't the first time, Mr. Flin?"

Bulnes said, "That, my dear friends, is what we're trying to find out. Could we check by geography?"

"How?" inquired Flin.

"Let's say by changes in the coast line, or the degree of erosion of the hills."

"I don't see how. We have no very exact information on the state of such matters in Classical times. Even if we did, we have no precise maps or other data to guide us."

"Well, for example," persisted Bulnes, "is the Corinthian Canal in existence? It is in our times but not, I believe, in the fifth century B.C."

"It ain't," said Diksen. "Least, they got a boat-hauling service there for pulling ships on rollers over the isthmus. One of the boys on the force was telling me."

"That should settle it," said Flin.

Bulnes said, "My dear Wiyem, you're determined to make this phenomenon real at all costs. But if the Emp could restore all of Classical Greece down to the last temple, he could fill in the Corinthian Canal."

"Well then," said Flin, "how about animal life? Mr. Diksen said something about lions, but there haven't been any wild lions in Europe since Classical times."

"They got 'em in Thessalia and Makedonia," said Diksen.

Bulnes said, "That wouldn't do either. Vasil could stock the country with lions from some African game preserve."

"I have another idea," said Flin. "How about some form of life now extinct? Like the aurochs? How about that, Mr. Diksen?"

"What's an auroc?"

"The aurochs was the wild ox that used to roam the forests of Europe."

"You mean that big black wild bull with the long horns? Yeah, they got them too. We got the skull of one on the wall of the barracks."

"There you are!" cried Flin. "Not even Vasil's resources can bring an extinct species back to life. Hence this must be the real Periklean Age."

"Wrong again, I'm sorry to say," said Bulnes. "The aurochs was brought back to life by some zoologist back in the twentieth century. Forget the man's name."

"How in the name of heaven did he do that?"

"He crossbred various strains of domestic cattle partly descended from the aurochs and kept picking those most like the ancestral aurochs until he re-established the original stock. There's been a small herd in existence ever since. You can see some at the London Zoo."

"I never knew that," said Flin. "Too bad there isn't some species like the mammoth that would really settle the question."

"How about language?" asked Bulnes. "Do the pronunciation and syntax of these Greeks match those of the real ancient ones?"

Flin spread his hands. "How can I tell? Nobody made phonographic recordings of the speech of the time of Perikles, so we have to guess at their pronunciation, more or less. It sounds all right to me, but there's no way of checking it."

"I got an idea," said Diksen. "I once read about how the position of the stars keeps changing, so after a coupla thousand years the Big Dipper'll look like a frying pan."

"That's it!" exclaimed Flin. "You know astronomy from your navigating experiences, Knut. How about it?"

"Won't do," said Bulnes. "The change wouldn't be enough to settle the question. But you do give me an idea."

"What?" said the other two at once.

"The North Celestial Pole."

"What's that?" said Diksen. "The place right overhead?"

"No, the point in the sky around which the stars turn. It changes its position continually, making a complete circle in—I forget exactly—something like twenty-five thousand years. If I could find an astronomer with some simple instruments, I could determine whether the Pole is now near Alpha Ursae Minoris or Alpha Draconis, or what. Not even Vasil the Ninth could change the inclination of the earth's axis for purposes of historical research. Who's an astronomer, Wiyem?"

"Oh dear me. I'm supposed to be a Greek scholar and all that rot, but without my reference books I don't know the ruddy subject as well as I thought. Anaxagoras might still be alive, and let's see—there was some other chap trying to reform the calendar. Can't think of his name. Not Myron, that's the sculptor, but something like that. Could you look into it, Mr. Diksen?"

"You want I should find an astronomer with a name something like Myron, huh?"

"That's it."

"Meanwhile, my dear friends," said Bulnes, "there's the little matter of making our livings, because this Athenian silver won't last forever."

"In the stories," said Flin, "the chappie who's tossed back in time makes his fortune by teaching the natives to add or inventing the airplane."

"I wouldn't try that," said Diksen. "These Gricks ain't got no idea of the usefulness of machinery so long as they got a lot of poor shmos to work as slaves. When my beat was on the Akropolis, I thought I'd save 'em trouble and get in with the right guys by suggesting wheelbarrows to haul their loads. What thanks do I get? 'Barbarian, you keep your goddam nose out of what don't concern you. We Gricks is the only people can think, and we don't need no advice from no low-down slave. Now get going.' Boy, I coulda wrapped my bow around that guy's neck. Bigshot architect, name of Iktinos."

"We seem to have a complete cast of characters in any event," said Flin. "D'you know Aspasia?"

"Yeah, sure—that is, I know who she is."

"Sokrates?"

"The funny-looking bald guy, always picking arguments in the Agora? Yeah."

"Protagoras?"

"Nope."

"Kleon the Tanner?"

"Maybe I heard of him. Not sure."

"Pheidias?"

"Nope."

After Flin had gone through several more names, most of which Diksen did not know, Bulnes said, "The question of making a living remains unsettled, but I think Mr. Diksen is right, that we should get nowhere trying to invent ourselves into affluence. I certainly couldn't invent the airplane. I have neither the engineering training nor the tools nor the materials."

"I don't think it's important," said Flin. "If I

find Thalia, I'll jolly well set out for the nearest frontier and take my chances on getting through."

"Until we get some personal security I don't see how we can hunt effectively for your wife, even assuming she's in this time stream or whatever you call it. Don't they keep the women shut up in harems here?"

"Yeah, they do," said Diksen. "Like they used to do in them Oriental countries."

"What's your suggestion, then?" said Flin.

Bulnes said, "If need be, we shouldn't be afraid of manual labor."

"Slave competition would keep wages down to the starvation level. However, if you become reasonably fluent in Classical Greek, why shouldn't we set up as sophists?"

"You mean those guys that lecture?" said Diksen.

"Absolutely. They were big business at the time, and were laying the foundations for higher education as we know it. We could give the people the Copernican system . . ."

"It seems to me," said Bulnes, "they used to feed hemlock poison to sophists who taught radical new ideas."

"Oh, we shall have to be careful."

"I think perhaps you've hit it," said Bulnes. "Mr. Diksen, how would it be if we hid out here a few days while our beards grow and we practice our Greek? Meanwhile you can hunt up this astronomer fellow."

"Sure. This guy here's Kallingos, and for a Grick innkeeper he's almost honest. I'll drop back down in about a week. If you want to look me up before then, come to the barracks on the Areopagos when I'm off duty." Diksen yawned. "Got to catch up on my sleep. So long!"

SEVEN

". . . in the indicative mood," said Flin implacably, "the secondary tenses are augmented."

"Why?" asked Bulnes.

"How on earth should I know? They are, that's all. Now this augment may be syllabic, by prefixing *epsilon* to verbs beginning with a consonant—or temporal, by lengthening an initial short vowel. Thus *paideuo,* 'I teach,' in the imperfect becomes *epaideuon,* 'I was teaching' . . ."

Flin broke off as Bulnes grasped his wrist, saying, "Did you see that tough-looking party talking to our host?"

"Yes. He's gone out now."

"I didn't like the look he gave us."

Bulnes shifted to his rudimentary Classical Greek. He had found that by throwing in a word of modern Greek when he could not think of the

Classical form, he could sometimes make himself understood. "O Kallingos!"

"You called?"

"Mine dear fellow, shall you not—ah—share cup of you—uh—excellent wine at us?"

"What said you?"

Bulnes repeated the offer with even greater care.

"Nai," said the innkeeper, wagging his head and confusing Bulnes until the latter remembered that this meant "yes." "O Bouleus, you are as polite as a Mede, though not so stupid. Boy! Another cup. You should not, however, call this Attic bellywash 'excellent.' If I could sell you a jar of my Lesbian . . ."

"What's he saying?" Bulnes asked Flin, who translated.

Bulnes gathered his mental forces and replied: "Me fear not—no got enough money. Whom—uh—who am—the man er—what's the word, Wiyem?"

"The man with whom you were speaking," said Flin.

"Not the kind of man," replied Kallingos, "you like to talk about."

"What's that, Wiyem? . . . Who this man, please?"

Kallingos lowered his voice. "Phaleas the son of Kniphon."

Bulnes and Flin exchanged glances. The latter said, "Didn't Diksen say something about Phaleas's gang?"

"Could be he." Bulnes turned to Kallingos. "Are him—er—ah—uh . . ."

"The noted criminal," put in Flin.

Kallingos looked over his shoulder. "He is. He says two members of his band were slain four nights ago by a pair of barbarians, and he is now looking for these killers to revenge himself. They were huge, powerful men in some hideous Scythian or Persian costume, wearing curious caps upon their heads and tunics and trousers cut and sewn to cling to their bodies closely. Some of the band were enjoying a game of knucklebones when these giants sprang out of the dark, stabbed two to death, and would have done in the rest had they not run away."

Bulnes continued with Flin's linguistic help, "Things have come at such a pass, poor thief cannot—ah—earn dishonest living in Peiraieus without—uh—being rob by more big thief."

"True, ha-ha. That was the same night that the mysterious ship appeared in Zea Harbor."

"What mysteriously ship?"

"Have you not heard? The state galley *Paralos* was caught by the storm on her way back from Epidauros and rode it out behind Salamis. When the wind fell she made a run for home and was feeling her way into Zea when she struck a strange ship that had taken her usual anchorage. The ship sank near the wharves, and can be dimly seen lying on the bottom even now, with sails of strange cut mounted all awry. There is some talk of sending divers down to fasten ropes to the hull."

"To raise she?" asked Bulnes, concealing his eagerness.

"Zeus, no! What use have we for an outlandish

rig like that? They will tow her into deeper water where she will not interfere with navigation. But now barbershops buzz with speculation as to whether there might not be a connection between these two events."

"I see . . . O friend Kallingos, I fear we must leaves tomorrow."

"What did you say?"

Bulnes repeated.

"I am sorry. Is there aught you like not?"

There were a lot of things, thought Bulnes, beginning with the bugs in the dormitory. But he said, "No, it are that we am going at Athens."

"*What?*" cried Flin in English. Bulnes ignored him.

"It is too bad you could not stay over tomorrow."

"Why?" said Bulnes.

"It is the day of the Dionysia," said Kallingos.

"What is being shown?" asked Flin.

"The *Aias* of Sophokles and two other plays, at our own Dionysiac Theater. As Euripides is not competing this year, the *Aias* may win."

"I say!" said Flin. "I shouldn't care to miss . . ."

"Shut up, my dear Wiyem," said Bulnes. "Will them play be show again anywhere?"

"Yes, at the regular Dionysia in Athens. Of course, as foreigners, you would have to pay to get in."

"We may see him then. Meanwhile, could you recommend us to a innkeeper in Athens as honest like you?"

Kallingos made a gesture. "To be frank, there is none in Attika so honest as I. Wherever else you go you will be deceived. If you ask for your wine diluted with one part of water, you will get it cut with two. However, you will not be too badly robbed at the inn of Podokles, a few houses east of the Agora.''

Bulnes thanked Kallingos, got some advice about prices from him, and went up to the dormitory, where Flin burst out, "What d'you mean by making a plan like that without consulting me? The logical thing is to exhaust the Peiraieus looking for Thalia before we think of moving. We've got a good innkeeper . . .''

"But this gang . . .'' said Bulnes.

Flin, however, though usually timid in the face of physical risk, now showed the unreasonable obstinacy with which weak men sometimes try to assert themselves. Bulnes let him run down and said, "I'm going tomorrow, my dear fellow. You may do as you like.''

When the eastern sky began to lighten, Bulnes groaned and forced himself up. He would never get used to the fiendishly early hours of the Athenians. They munched their sops and paid up. Flin said no more about refusing to move to Athens, and Bulnes refrained from taunting him.

Bulnes noted that Kallingos tried to swindle them out of only two or three oboloi—for an Attic innkeeper, he supposed, comparative rectitude. Then, as the sun gilded the brass helmet of Athene Promachos on the Akropolis the two travelers gathered their himatia about them and set out upon the dusty road to Athens, Bulnes muttering the paradigms of irregular verbs.

Flin said, "There should be a road running

north of the Long Walls. It would give us a good
view of the country, while between the Walls we
shan't see anything."

"Anything you say, my dear comrade."

They pushed to northward through the stirring
seaport toward the gate adjacent to the junction of
the North Long Wall and the Peiraic Wall. After
passing through the gate they came upon the
muddy Kephisos in full spring spate, not yet
shrunken with the summer drouth. The highway
crossed the river by a ford.

Bulnes sighed. "Here, my friend, it seems we
get wet."

Flin gathered up his himation, growling, "Jolly
unfortunate we didn't land in a later century
when they'd have had a bridge."

They splashed into the broad calf-deep crossing, climbed out the far side, and trudged up the
hard-beaten wagon track across the flat Attic
plain. Most of the plain was a waste of new grass
and wild flowers, with a few stands of wheat and
clumps of gray-green olive trees in the hollows.
Other roads, even more rudimentary, joined
theirs at intervals. Along these roads, mostly toward Athens, moved a traffic of vegetables, hides,
firewood, and similar commodities. This traffic,
sometimes on the backs of donkeys and sometimes on those of men, thickened as they neared
the city.

After more than an hour the road confusingly
began to fork and rejoin itself as they neared the
walls of Athens. (Not, thought Bulnes, a very impressive defense.) On a flat space in front of the
wall a group of men with shields, spears, and
crested helmets marched back and forth.

Stopping to draw breath and watch, Bulnes remarked, "They don't look much like Greek gods, do they?"

They did not, for the Athenian militiamen came in the usual range of human sizes and shapes, tall and short, fat and thin. Although the universal beards and cheek-plates of the helmets lent them a deceptive similarity, a close look showed that they varied about as much in features as a random group of modern southern Europeans. Like the Greeks of Bulnes's own time they were mostly brunets, tending toward a stocky build.

Flin sighed. "I confess I find them something of a disappointment. Perhaps we shall be more impressed when we get to the Agora."

They followed the crowd through the nearest gate, a complex structure intended as a practical defense, for it included two sets of doors with a passage between them overlooked by galleries. A little group of Scythian archers watched the traffic and straightened out tangles.

Inside, a street about five meters wide led in the direction of the Akropolis. The city itself, however, proved far from impressive: a huddle of one-storey mud-brick buildings with the same blank, windowless outer walls that Bulnes had noticed in the Peiraieus. Here, moreover, instead of being laid out in a rectangular grid, the houses were placed every which way. The streets were nothing but crooked little alleys winding among the houses, often barely wide enough to let two pedestrians pass, with no pavements anywhere. The stench was worse than at the seaport. Out of this noisome confusion rose the Akropolis, crowned with marble and bronze, like a tiara on a garbage heap, with the peak of Mount Lykabettos towering behind it.

Bulnes, feeling that Flin knew the terrain from his studies, let his companion lead the way. Flin tended to get lost in rapturous contemplation of the objects around him.

"Come, my dear comrade," said Bulnes. "We're hunting the inn of Podokles. Remember?"

Flin shook his head, as if awakening, and led the way onward. Presently the street opened out into the Agora, like that of the Peiraieus, but bigger. It proved to be an open space in name only, for in addition to the statues, monuments, and plane trees that dotted it, it was crammed with tradesmen's kiosks.

The space left among these structures was crowded with Athenians, all reeking of garlic, waving their hands, shouting, laughing, haggling, arguing, and shaking fists in each other's faces. Many wore violets in their hair—"In honor of the Dionysia," Flin explained.

Flin pushed sunward through the crowd; Bulnes, towering over the short Greeks, strolled after him, wishing he had pants pockets to thrust his hands into.

"Looking for somebody?" asked Bulnes.

"My wife, of course. And I thought we might catch sight of Sokrates or Prodikos."

"My dear fellow! We don't even know yet if it's the real Sokrates or a modern imitation, and in any case I doubt if you could recognize him. There are enough bald, potbellied men here to make a hundred Sokratai." Bulnes turned and spoke to a passing Athenian. *"To pandokeion Podoklou?"*

"What?"

"*To pandokeion Podoklou?*"

"I know not," said the man, and went his way.

As they worked over toward the east side of the Agora they repeated their question until they got a set of directions, but with so much pointing and arm waving that the inn might have lain anywhither. Another half-hour's search and more questions brought them to their goal in the Limoupedion district.

Podokles proved a burly fellow with part of his nose missing from a sword cut. "Foreigners, eh? Where are you from?"

Bulnes had expected Flin to carry the burden of negotiations, but the teacher was lost in the contemplation of the design on a jar. So Bulnes told Podokles, "Tartessos. I be Bouleus and him Philon."

"Where is that?"

"In Far West."

"What did you say?"

"To the West."

"You mean Sicily?"

"Farther."

"Hm. I thought beyond Sicily was nothing but shoals and sea monsters. Know you anybody in Athens? I have to be careful."

Hardly the genial host, thought Bulnes. "Kallingos at Peiraieus referred us to you. We stayed with he."

"Then you may be all right," said Podokles dubiously, and they argued terms for a quarter-hour.

Bulnes handed Podokles the bag containing

their modern clothes (recovered from the arsenal)
and their few other possessions, and asked,
"When are lunch?"

"Name of the Dog, you fellows get hungry early! If you want anything prepared, go buy it and
bring it to my cook."

Bulnes said to Flin, "I can't get used to beginning the day at dawn. Let's look up Diksen."

"What are you two babbling about?" said
Podokles.

"Not you, my dear friend," said Bulnes, smiling
blandly through his stubble.

. They went out and trudged through the filth
toward the Hill of Ares, looking around to be sure
of finding their way back. On the hill itself they
passed a shed containing a curious object: a ship
mounted on wagon wheels, used (Flin explained)
in certain religious processions. At last they came
to the barracks.

Roi Diksen, alias Pardokas, came out of the barracks rubbing the sleep out of his eyes. "I didn't
expect to see you two for several days yet!"

Bulnes told him of the activities of Phaleas the
gangster.

"Uh-huh," said Diksen. "I'd like to pin something on that ganef, but I think he's bought protection from one of the big shots. Can you make
with the Grick, now?"

"Enough to manage if not to compete with the
orators. Have you found our astronomer?"

"Yeah, just yesterday. Old geezer, name of Meton, lives just off the Agora."

"Splendid!" said Bulnes. "We thank you most
gratefully."

"Aw . . . Us barbarians got to stick together, see?"

"Meton!" said Flin. "By Jove, I remember now: He's the chap who burned—I mean he *will* burn his house down in—umm—fifteen or twenty years so that the Assembly will order his son to stay home from the Sicilian expedition to take care of him."

Bulnes looked questioningly at Flin. "How do we get access to this Meton?"

"That would take a bit of doing, you know. An Athenian citizen's home is his castle."

"Yeah," said Diksen. "Back in Yonkers, you wanna ask some guy something, you call him up and ask him, or say can you come around and see him? But these Gricks is funny. You knock on their door as polite as anything and if you ain't a citizen they sick the dog on you. Foreigners like you and slaves like me is just dirt under their feet."

Bulnes asked, "Does Meton ever go to the Agora?"

"Naw. Just sits around diddling with his calendars and things."

Bulnes said, "I suppose we shall have to find someone who can tender the proper introductions. It's like the story of the two Englishmen wrecked on a desert island who never spoke to each other until they were rescued, seven years later, because there was nobody present who could properly introduce them."

"A base canard," said Flin. "Don't believe him, Mr. Diksen. The English are as affable as anybody."

"I wish you luck," said Diksen, "but I can't help you none. An introduction from a slave wouldn't be no recommendation."

Bulnes said, "At least you could tell us where to find Sokrates in the Agora."

"I guess he mostly hangs out around the *Basileios Stoa*, or one of them places. Now can I go back to sleep?"

Bulnes and Flin left the pseudo-Scythian and walked back down the slope of the Areopagos. Flin, wistfully eyeing the Akropolis a mere hundred meters away over his shoulder, said, "You don't suppose we could take an hour off for a spot of sight-seeing."

"No, my dear Wiyem, I don't. Sokrates first."

"We can at least take this street that runs down to the south end of the Agora and get a look at the things along the north side of the Akropolis . . . That building must be the Thesmothetaion—or would it be the Prytaneion? Dash it all, I wish I had an eidetic memory . . ."

"Why not ask?" said Bulnes.

"And accost some total stranger? Ah, there's something I know. See those holes in the cliff?"

"Yes."

"They're the caves of Pan and Apollo. There are supposed to be secret stairs or passages leading from them up to the Akropolis . . . And there are the Long Rocks—those are the statues of the Tribal Heroes, and those are the public bulletin boards—"

"Excuse me, comrade, but you're taking us away from our destination."

"So I am," sighed Flin.

Back at the Agora they soon located the Royal Stoa among the shops and offices along the west side of the plaza. Inside the building, a crowd of people watched an argument being conducted before a man who sat on a raised seat and wore a purple himation and a dried-up wreath on his head.

"That," said Flin, "must be the King."

"I thought this was a republic?"

"It is, but they've kept the kingship as a sort of vestigial office. As I recall, he's a combination high-priest and domestic-relations judge."

"I see. Please start asking people for Sokrates."

"Dash it all, you know I hate speaking to strangers. Why don't you? You need the practice."

"Oh, all right—for you I will. But kindly listen to their replies and be prepared to translate. When they speak fast, I get lost." Knut Bulnes turned his best Greek on one of his immediate neighbors, "Have you see Sokrates, please?"

Within a quarter-hour he had collected a variety of replies: "What?" "No." "I do not know the man." "Do you mean Sokrates the carpenter?" "I have never heard of him." "What are you saying?" "Not today." "I do not understand you." "He and his questions! When I catch that scoundrel . . ." "I am a stranger, too." "No, and if you find him, tell him Mnesiphilos wants his five drachmai back." "Who are you?" And finally, "You are looking in the wrong place. He is usually to be found in the *Stoa Poikile.*"

"Thank you," said Bulnes, and turned to Flin. "Where now?"

"I think the Painted Porch was—is—across the

Agora. And if you expect to pass as an Athenian,
you'll have to drop those ceremonious manners.
The average Athenian has no more manners than
an American."

"Really, my dear fellow? Most of the people I
met in the United States had adequate manners . . ."

They pushed out into the noonday glare, stopping at the Bread Market long enough to buy a big
loaf from a truculent old woman for three coppers,
but passing up a vendor of hot water for drinking
at an obolos and a half a cup. Though Bulnes
hungrily eyed a sausage-seller's stock, Flin objected, "Probably give you trichinosis. Anyway,
this bread's so full of garlic and things it has all
the vitamins we need."

As they walked, munching, a beggar plucked at
the himation of Bulnes and whined. The man had
a missing foot, an empty eyesocket, and some
loathsome skin affliction, so Bulnes gave him a
copper. Instantly a swarm of beggars descended
upon the pair, clutching and importuning.

"Now you've done it!" cried Flin, and shouted
"Go away!" until the beggars dispersed. "Why
d'you do things like that? We're nearly in the
gazette ourselves."

"I suppose I'm a soft touch," said Bulnes. "We
see so few beggars I haven't developed an immu-
nity to them. In Italy I could always get rid of
people trying to sell me things by saying 'Ich will
nicht,' but I don't know what would work here."

They won through the mob to the Painted
Porch, where Flin gabbled over the murals: one of
the Battle of Marathon, one of the Sack of Troy,

one of Theseus fighting the Amazons, and one of some other battles. Bulnes admitted, "The execution's not too bad, but they can't have known anything about perspective. Gives a grotesque effect, don't you think?"

He resumed the questioning of passers-by about Sokrates until Flin plucked at his cloak, saying, "Over there. Looks like a sophist with his pupils."

A dignified-looking graybeard was sitting on a bench and lecturing three younger men. Bulnes went up behind the hearers and held up his hand until the lecturer interrupted himself, "Yes? You wish something?"

"Thousand pardons, sir, but have you see Sokrates?"

"What is that?"

"I said, have you see Sokrates?"

One of the youths said something nasty about barbarians who sought wisdom before they could even speak Greek, and the other two laughed. However, the graybeard cut through the ribaldry. "No, my good man, for he is not in Athens today."

"Indeed?"

"In fact he has gone off on a picnic, to revel with the nymphs and satyrs on Mount Hymettos, with Perikles's nephew Alkibiades. You may find him back here tomorrow. Where was I? Ah, yes . . . whereas the Philolaos has been asserting the world to be a sphere, this speculation is shown to be absurd and untenable by . . ."

"Now can we visit the Akropolis? Can we?" said Flin.

"Very well, my dear comrade."

They walked back to the south end of the Agora

and thence to the path that wound up the west end
of the Akropolis, through the Propylaia or entrance, and out at last on to the flat top of the great
ship-shaped hill, about three hundred meters
long and half as wide. With each step Flin's condition became more ecstatic until he broke into a
run, dashing from statue to statue as if his life
depended upon his seeing everything at once. He
babbled happily, "That's the great Athene Promachos, Knut, though the name only goes back . . .
A Pheidias original! Think of it!"

He put out a finger and delicately touched the
brazen foot of the ten-meter colossus.

"Looks bovine to me," said Bulnes. "I thought
some of those others were prettier."

Flin, as if he had not heard, was reading the
dedicatory inscription on a huge ornamental
bronze chariot, almost big enough to have been
pulled by elephants: ". . . the spoils taken from
the Boiotians and Euboians . . ."

He moved on to where a group of workmen
were planting a life-sized statue of Athene on its
pedestal, with ropes and grunts. "And this must
be Myron's group of Athene and Marsyas, only
Marsyas isn't mounted yet. Excuse me," he said to
an elderly man directing operations, "but are you
Myron?"

"Why yes," said the man.

Flin shut his eyes and squeezed his hands together. "I've seen Myron! I've seen Myron! Isn't it
the most dashed wonderful thing you ever saw,
Knut? I don't care if I die tomorrow, now I've seen
this! Come on, there's the Parthenon!"

And off he galloped, sandals flapping. "No, the
entrance is around the far end."

"Why," asked Bulnes, "should they put the entrance at the east end when you come up on to the Akropolis from the west?"

"Some religious reason, or perhaps they wanted the rising sun to light the statue inside for dawn ceremonies. Isn't it beautiful? Isn't it gorgeous?"

Bulnes said, "I must say the Akropolis looks different from what I expected. All those bright colors give the effect of one of the gaudier American amusement parks."

"Didn't you know they painted their temples and statues? I hope after all we've gone through it's the real original Akropolis and not a modern imitation, like that one in Nashville or whatever that American city is."

EIGHT

Three hours later they slouched into the inn of Podokles. Bulnes said, "I've got museum feet, and I think a nice big mug of wine—thank you, my dear Podokles. Wiyem, if you find yourself broke in Athens, you can make a living as a tourist guide. But don't try to show everything at once. I've seen so many statues they all look alike to me."

"I suppose I did let my enthusiasm run away with me," said Flin humbly. He made a face at his wine. "Hang it all, if I could only have a dish of tea!"

"Wrong century."

"Uh-huh. I admit the sheer physical discomfort of this environment does take some of the bloom off."

"Personally," said Bulnes, "I shall be satisfied

hereafter to view ancient Greece in the form of
museum exhibits.''

"Oh, but you don't get the same effect at all!''
Flin took a gulp of his wine, spilling a little out of
the wide shallow cup, more like a soup plate on a
base than a proper drinking vessel. "If you'll come
up on the Akropolis again, I'll show you the
other . . .''

"God forbid! Podokles, my friend, give us of
your wisdom. How is Periklean regime doing?''

The innkeeper, thawing to Bulnes's persistent
friendliness, planted his broad bottom on the
bench. "Not too well.''

"How so?''

"Everybody expected war and was full of enthusiasm. Then the Perikles suddenly made a
treaty with the Spartans, compromised with the
Corinthians, and offered the Potidaians synoe-
cism.''

"Offered them what?''

"Common citizenship with Athens. A lot of the
commercial people are saying: Why go to all the
trouble of building up an empire if we are to give
its benefits away to foreigners? What do you
think?''

"I fear as foreigners my friend and I is prej-
udice.''

"What?''

"Never mind. What will come of these?''

"I do not know. I fear that if the Perikles con-
tinues to follow a soft line in foreign affairs, the
radical factions will join with the extreme conser-
vatives to gain control of the Assembly. I, now, am
for moderation, wherefore I have always favored
the Perikles.''

"So that's how it was!" said Flin.

"We don't know yet," said Bulnes, and to Podokles: "How do the radicals propose attack Perikles?"

"There is a rumor—Polites Eurybotou was repeating it here the other night—that Dophithes and Kleon and those fellows were going after his friends, since he himself is too popular. They think they have something on some of them."

Flin exclaimed, "Then it is real! It must be! Because that's just what happened. We've got to warn Perikles they're after Pheidias and Anaxagoras and Aspasia!"

"Take it easy, my dear fellow," said Bulnes. "What shall they do to Perikles' friends?"

"Indictments," said Podokles. "For instance, the Pheidias handled a lot of gold in his work on the New Hekatompedon of Athene Polias . . ."

"The which?"

Flin interjected, "What you'd call the Parthenon. Go on, Podokles."

"As I was saying, he handled much gold in doing the work, and it would be surprising if some had not stuck to his fingers."

Later Flin told Bulnes, "This waiting is driving me mad. Here we're running out of money with no more in sight. My wife is God knows where. The plot against Perikles is gathering. And we sit waiting for Sokrates to come back."

"You can't rush things like that without ruining them. And what makes you so sure we want to save Perikles?"

"The Peloponnesian War ruined Hellenic culture . . ."

"I thought Aristotle and a lot of other important thinkers came after this war?"

"They did, but—oh, it's too complicated to explain. Political morality had broken down and so on. Evidently Perikles tried to stave off the war, but the rabble-rousers forced his hand by attacking his associates—so he dropped his efforts to conciliate Sparta and let the war break out to unite the people behind him. Now if we could only . . ."

"My dear friend, we don't even know yet if this is the genuine Perikles. Even assuming we're back in ancient times, what should we accomplish? Perhaps we should find ourselves unable to change anything, since an act once done can hardly be undone. Or if we did change events, we should alter all subsequent history and destroy ourselves in the process."

"Nonsense! We haven't disappeared yet. We might start history off on another tack . . ."

"So men would perfect the solar bomb in the third century instead of the twentieth and, having no notion of a world society, would merrily blow each other off the face of the globe? Let's wait till we have all the facts."

Next morning found them scouring the Agora until, several hours after sunrise, a disturbance around the Painted Porch drew their attention. There stood a new arrival among the talkers and loafers, a short, bald, potbellied, snub-nosed man of about forty, barefoot, wearing nothing but a ragged himation, whom it did not need the greetings of his acquaintances to identify as Sokrates.

Though most of the chatter was too fast for Bulnes to follow, he caught a reference to Sokrates's previous day.

"Of course," said Sokrates, "you will understand that my affection for the young Alkibiades is of a purely spiritual kind."

The dignified graybeard of the previous day was there too, saying, "Rejoice, O Sokrates!" with the rest.

"Rejoice, O Protagoras," said Sokrates. "I heard you were in Athens and hastened to see you. How long will you be with us this time?"

"Perhaps a month. Have you seen Demokritos?"

"I know him not. Is he in Athens, too?"

"He set out before I did, and should be here unless he has been lost at sea."

"Well, we have not seen him hereabouts," said Sokrates.

Flin breathed, "That was Protagoras we spoke to yesterday! I never thought we should run into anybody really *important* just like that!"

"Who the devil's Protagoras?" asked Bulnes.

"Such ignorance! He's—oh, hush up and listen!"

Sokrates continued, "Are you giving courses, Protagoras?"

"A brief one to pay my traveling expenses."

"How do you expect the purity of philosophy to withstand the contamination of vulgar commercial transactions?"

"As to that, Sokrates, I am not aware of any rule that philosophers have not the same right to eat as other men. Therefore I charge."

"Therefore you consider your teachings worth money?"

"Certainly," replied Protagoras.

"But I remember on your last visit, when we argued whether virtue could be taught, you professed that your teachings were priceless. If they are priceless, you obviously cannot put a price upon them."

"I do not. As I explained, I really charge for my time. The teachings are free."

"But how can you distinguish the time from the teachings, since the teachings take time to expound, and are therefore in a sense the same as the time?"

"Sokrates, you are an amusing rascal and I am glad to see you, but I will be ground to sausage and fed to Kerberos before I let you entrap me in one of your quibbles again."

"Be not angry. I admit I am an ignorant man in search of wisdom, and here you come, the godlike Protagoras, all the way from windy Abdera to dispense it, so naturally I make the most of my oppor—"

"Excuse me," said Protagoras firmly. "I see a couple of strangers who were asking for you yesterday. Come forward, sirs, and give your names."

"Me?" said Bulnes, a little disconcerted. "I am—uh—Bouleus of Tartessos, and my friend am Philon of Tartessos."

"Can you understand him?" said one onlooker to another. Bulnes persisted, "Hearing you were—ah—wisest man in Athens, Sokrates, we sought you out to make selves better."

Sokrates smiled an embarrassed grin. "No, no,

somebody has been filling you with lies. My only advantage is that I know I am ignorant, whereas the other simpletons do not." He did not, however, sound displeased by the flattery.

"Tartessos?" said Protagoras. "Is that not in Spain, at the very rim of the known world?"

"It is," said Bulnes.

"I thought that city was either destroyed by the Carthaginians or sunk beneath the sea by an earthquake, back about the Seventieth Olympiad. I have heard both tales."

Bulnes, whose knowledge of historical geography was slight, turned to Flin. The little Englishman stepped into the breach, "True, Tartessos is not what it was, but it has not been destroyed. It has decayed because the silting up of the Tartessis River has left it stranded among great mudflats, so that it is no longer accessible to large ships."

"I see," said Protagoras. "Are the stories of its former mineral wealth true?"

"Quite true. In fact, we Tartessians believe your poet Homeros based his Scheria, the city of the Phaiakes in the Odyssey, upon an account of Tartessos."

Protagoras smiled. "Evidently the Tartessians are feeling their way to the theory of my colleague Prodikos of Keos, that all myths are either personifications of natural forces or exaggerated versions of the deeds of mortal men. I must tell the Prodikos when I see him. You know, Sokrates, one of your Athenian rhapsodes like this Xenophanes could turn the tale of Tartessos into a fine pseudo-epic."

"How?" said Sokrates. "More poet's lies?"

"Oh, make Atlas the king of it—the mountain named for him is out there somewhere, is it not?—and tell how Zeus sank the golden city beneath the waters of the Outer Sea when its people became insolent in their success, leaving nothing but impassible shoals."

Flin started to explain. "You mean Plato's story of Atlant—" and stopped.

"Who is this Platon?" said Sokrates. "I do not know the story."

"He is not yet b— I mean, that is—uh . . ."

Bulnes stepped in. "Gentlemen: I will with you permission—ah—put up a puzzle to you. Let us suppose the world are inhabited by race of gods who powers are far beyond our. They can fly to the moon, talk to each other over thousands of stadia, and light their dwellings with lamp that require no oil. Let us suppose this gods can make men complete not only in body but also in mind, so that a man just made has a memory stretching all the way back to his nonexistent childhood. And let us suppose as an experiment these god set aside part of the earth called 'Hellas' and stock it with the present population of those lands, all with the necessary—er—pseudo-memories, and a complete outfit of buildings, ship, and the like. Now, let us suppose you are those people, and experiment started five or six years ago. How might you prove otherwise?"

"But," objected Protagoras, "I have a clear memory going back more years than I like to think."

"I explain that. How could you prove this not a

false memory implanted in you mind by the gods who made you six years ago?"

"Ridiculous," said a bystander.

Bulnes turned to the objector with his blandest smile. "No doubt, my dear fellow, but how would you prove?"

"There is no need to prove it. It just is."

"That what you call summary justice. What do the philosophers think?"

Sokrates said, "What happens when one of these newly made Hellenes set forth on a long journey, as when a Greek city sends people to found a colony in the Euxine Sea? They would come to the bounds of this Hellas and enter the country of the gods, so discovering themselves to be mere pets, like carp in a fish pond."

Bulnes said, "We shall suppose the gods put the traveler to sleep as he nears boundary and then awaken him at an appropriate time and set him on the route back to Hellas, with a set of false memories of him journey through barbarous lands."

"You mean," said Protagoras, "that such places as Egypt and Spain exist not, save as images implanted in our minds by these crafty gods of yours?"

"Perhaps, perhaps not. For all you know, my friend and I might be gods come to see how the experiment are going. Except if we were, we would not let you in on the secret so careless."

"I see," said Protagoras. "Very ingenious. In fact it agrees with what I have been preaching for years—that as all our knowledge comes through our fallible senses, reality may be vastly different from what it seems, because of the distortions of our perceiving apparatus."

Sokrates said, "I should agree, except that you do not allow for the direct inspiration of the soul by the divine powers. Otherwise, it is as if we were all prisoners sitting at the entrance to a cave, facing the far wall, with our heads so shackled that we could not move, and trying to make out what is happening in the world outside by the shadows thrown on the cave wall and the sounds of traffic and conversation behind us."

"A striking example, Sokrates," said Protagoras. "And now I must get back to my pupils. I shall see you again. Rejoice!"

Sokrates said to Bulnes, "Tartessos does produce acute reasoners, especially for a barbaric land. What do Tartessians hold to be the ultimate good?"

Bulnes, foreseeing an endless argument, said, "That depends on the men, some seeking the satisfaction of their own appetites, some the good of their fellows, and some the advancement of knowledges. As for us, we are so ignorant as you say yourself to be, and hope you will enlighten us. What does you think?"

"Oh, I am without doubt the most ignorant man in all Hellas! You should have asked the Protagoras. He knows all the answers, and will gladly convey them to you at fifty drachmai a day. However, now that you have asked me, I will try to demonstrate the identity of the good, the true, and the beautiful . . ."

"One moment, O Sokrates!" said Bulnes in some alarm. "Before you begin, do you know Meton the astronomer?"

"Why yes, I know him, and Anaxagoras and Archelaos and all that crew. When I was interested in such matters, I consorted with them regularly, before I decided upon the futility of all material science. The true astronomer, I now maintain, should have no need to spend his nights on his roof gazing at the stars, catching a cold in his head and a crick in his neck. He should derive the laws of the universe by pure logic. For, reason is the only infallible sense possessed by man. The others are fallible and delusive, and when applied to the vulgar and imperfect things of this material world . . ."

"True," interrupted Bulnes, "but we wondered if—that is, you could do us a great favor by introducing us to Meton. As foreigners, you know, we cannot walk up to him front door and . . ."

"What do you want to know that fellow for? All his stargazing and calendar-calculating have not made one wife more faithful, or one politician more honest. Such prying into divine secrets never meant for mortals to know is sheer insanity. Now, as I was saying . . ."

"Because," persisted Bulnes, "while your wisdom is without doubt of a more fundamental and significant kind, the city of Tartessos, when he sent us forth, told us to look him up to ask him some questions about geography and such matters."

"Are you free men?" said Sokrates. "I do not see your slaves."

"We are."

Flin added, "As I understand it, to have legal protection while here we must enroll with the Polemarchos as registered metics and get some

citizen to stand as our patron. Now, if you—
ahem—could see your way . . ."

"Nothing easier," said Sokrates. "But as I was
saying about the good, nothing is simply good in
relation to nothing. Everything must be good for
something, or the reverse, and thus a thing can be
both good and bad, depending upon . . ."

Not daring to interrupt again, Bulnes gritted his
teeth to listen.

Six hours later, Sokrates glanced at the lower-
ing sun. "By the Dog of Egypt! I have talked the
day through without stopping even to eat. You
poor fellows must be starved!"

"While the meat of your discourse is adequate
nourishment," said Bulnes, "I admit the clamor of
the material man begin to drown out the divine
thoughts of the spiritual one."

"Which brings up the question of dinner. Boy!"

A young man sitting on the ground with his
back to a pillar and dozing now got up and
wrapped himself in a himation even more ragged
than that of Sokrates. Bulnes realized with a slight
shock that this must be Sokrates's personal slave;
he had not thought of the philosopher as a slave-
owner.

Sokrates said, "Two days ago I spent my last
obolos for a meal for Dromon and myself, and
hence must depend upon my friends until my
next rents come in. Being a bachelor, I have no
wife to cook for me in any case."

"Oh!" said Bulnes. "You must allow us! While
fare at our inn are not that of Persian kings . . ."

"A kind offer," said Sokrates, "but I have a

better idea. Whom did you wish to meet? Meton? Let us therefore sponge on him for dinner!''

And the philosopher set off at a pace that made the short Flin pant, and forced even Bulnes to stretch his long legs.

NINE

Sokrates banged the door of Meton's house with his stick and roared, "Boy! Boy!"

When the spy hole opened and a wrinkled face appeared, the philosopher added, "Tell your master the greatest dunce in Athens is here with two other ninnies from far countries."

The hole closed and after a while opened again, to disclose a man older than Sokrates but younger than Protagoras—a thin man with a sharp, glittering-eyed expression.

"O Sokrates!" said the man. "I have not seen you since the banquet at the house of Alkamenes last year, when you got drunk and danced the kordax."

"I am never drunk! Besides, you were asleep under your couch at the time and could not see what I was dancing."

"And who are these?" said Meton.

"My new acquaintances from far Tartessos. You will find them quite gentlemanly even though they be not Hellenes, let alone Athenians." Sokrates introduced them, adding, "They say they have an astronomical problem for you."

"Come in, come in, do not stand there like so many herms," said Meton. He turned and shouted back over his shoulder, "E! You women, out of there!"

There was a twitter of female voices and a scrambling sound. Bulnes started to follow Sokrates through the vestibule, but was stopped by Meton, who said in a marked manner, "Are you not going to leave your shoes?"

"I is sorry," he said, and doffed his sandals before following Meton into the open court at the end of the passage.

The court was nothing but a bare rectangle of beaten earth with an altar in the middle, from which a thread of incense smoke arose. The barren patch was surrounded by wooden columns holding up the inner edge of the roof; and the columns in turn were encompassed by a lot of dark little curtained cells opening onto the court. In the courtyard stood a table on which was spread a mass of sheets of papyrus held down by a stone for a paperweight. In one corner a very old man sat at a smaller table, working on some similar sheets.

"Rejoice, Anaxagoras!" Sokrates called across the court to the oldster, who replied in kind.

"What is your problem, men of Tartessos?" asked Meton.

Bulnes had been composing sentences in anticipation of this question. He said, "You—uh—know the theory, Meton, that the earth is round like a ball?"

"What did you say?"

Bulnes repeated.

"Yes, of course," said Meton. "The silly Pythagoreans have been making that claim for several years, and I begin to think they have hit upon the right answer by the wrong method. It would explain many things, such as the shape of the earth's shadow during eclipses of the moon."

"What do you mean, silly Pythagoreans?" said Sokrates. "Perhaps you, who know so much more than I, would condescend to explain wherein lies the silliness of their divine teachings?"

"Their approach, my dear Sokrates, is entirely unscientific: number mysticism, intuition, and all that moonshine. By the way," and Meton sent a sharp look at Bulnes, "I trust you two foreigners are not here to spread that pernicious Babylonian superstition that is ruining scientific astronomy?"

"What do you mean, sir?" said Bulnes.

"Oh, that species of astronomical divination that pretends that the stars control our destinies here on earth and can be used for purposes of prophecy."

"Not at all," said Bulnes.

Sokrates said, "My good Meton, this materialistic so-called science of yours is bankrupt, and you might as well admit it. You and your colleagues have gazed at the stars and plucked at lyre-strings and tried to weigh smoke in a bag, and you have come to a dead end. The material senses alone can

do no more for you. If you would seek divine aid
in bettering your character, now . . ."

"Later, later," said Meton. "Let us finish with
these strangers first. What about the roundness of
the earth?"

Bulnes said, "We Tartessians believe if we can
get measurement of height of the North Celestial
Pole from the horizon in enough places, we shall
be materials for a complete—uh—complete—
what's the word, Wiyem?"

"Map."

"A complete map of the world."

"*Papai!* Now that is an idea," said Meton, making gestures with his fingers. "The angle from the
North Celestial Pole to the horizon will be the
same as the angle the observer stands at from the
equator toward the North Pole, would it not? A
neat point. O Anaxagoras!"

The old man looked up.

"Come here and take some notes. These men
have brought an interesting theorem with them."

Anaxagoras came over with a papyrus sheet
and wrote as Meton dictated.

"Are you really Anaxagoras of Klazomenai?"
asked Flin.

"Indeed I am," quavered the oldster. "Do the
Tartessians then know of the poor old
Anaxagoras, neglected of the world and sunk to a
pensioner of the generous Meton?"

"Nonsense!" gruffed Meton. "He enjoys feeling
sorry for himself. That is all for the present, old
man. Well then, Bouleus of Tartessos, what more
do you wish?"

"We thought if you had instruments at your

house, you might let us make observations of the position of the Pole to find it height here at Athens."

"Hm. That could be arranged. I tell you, come back here this evening after dinner and we will take a look from the roof. You will stay, will you not, Sokrates?"

"I shall not need much urging," said Sokrates. "Good-bye for the present, my foreign friends."

Bulnes said to Flin in English, "That's what in America they call the bum's rush." Then to Meton, "Many thanks, my dear sir. It is an honor to have meet you."

"Nonsense. It is no honor at all. Be back after dark, but do not keep me up all night waiting— what is it, Anaxagoras?"

The oldster had been plucking at Meton's chiton. Now he muttered into Meton's ear. After a whispered argument Meton said, "Anaxagoras asks me to invite you to stay so he can question you on the geography of Spain. He is always after such details to improve his world map, you know. How about it?"

Bulnes smiled broadly. "You are much too kind . . ."

"Of course, if you have an engagement . . ."

". . . but my colleague and I would not miss an hour in such learned company for anythings. We accept with heartfelt thanks."

Meton, looking none too pleased, turned to shout to a slave to set extra places. Anaxagoras laid a bony hand on the arms of Flin and Bulnes, saying, "If you will step into my room, my dear friends . . ."

The room turned out to be one of the airless, lightless cubicles opening on to the court. Anaxagoras thrust the curtain aside and ushered them in.

Inside, Bulnes saw, leaning against one wall, a huge rectangular sheet of papyrus in a wooden frame. On it was drawn a world map with Greece in the center of a great circular mass in which the Mediterranean, Red, and Caspian Seas made indentations from different directions. While Greece was drawn with fair accuracy, the other parts became less and less recognizable as one went outward from the center. After some puzzling, Bulnes made out that the tapering horn on the left extremity of Europe was supposed to represent the Iberian Peninsula.

He said, "With all due modesty, my dear Anaxagoras, I thinks I can improve on that. Have you something to draw with?"

Anaxagoras produced a piece of charcoal from the litter and said, "Draw on the wall, if you will."

Bulnes stared at the plaster (on which appeared the half-erased remains of other map sketches) for a few seconds while the picture of his native land formed in his mind. Then he drew rapidly, correcting by smudging out and redrawing once or twice, and adding the main courses of the Ebro, the Tajo, and the Guadalquivir. At the mouth of the last, in the lower left corner of Spain near where Cadiz should be, he drew a little circle.

"Tartessos," he said.

Anaxagoras whinnied with pleasure. "Many thanks! Many thanks! This is the greatest single addition to my map since I started work on it forty years ago. Know you any more of the coasts of the world's outer rim?"

Bulnes smiled and added the western and northern coasts of France. He said to Flin, "Suppose you put in the British Isles. You know them better than I." Then to Anaxagoras, "To you Hellenes of course it seem as though you lived at the center of the world and we at the outer rim, but to us it seem like we lived at the center and you at the far edge. It is all in point of view."

"You mean there are other lands beyond what we used to call the rim of the world?"

"Certainly. Whole continents unknown to you."

"By Hera! I work a lifetime on this map. I correct the blunders of Thales and Anaximandros and Hekataios, and just when I think it perfect, you fellows wander in from far places and blast my hopes with a single sentence. Such is life, I suppose. What is your friend drawing?"

Flin answered, "These are the Tin Islands, which you have perhaps heard of."

"Wonderful! Then the Western Ocean does in fact pass around to the North of Europe? Ha, would that Herodotos were in Athens! He doubts that such is the case. And how do you divide the continents of Europe and Asia?"

"Oh, we do not consider Europe a continent," said Flin, "but a mere peninsula on the continent of Asia—ouch! What are you kicking me for?"

The last sentence was in English to Bulnes, who replied with a suave smile, "Don't seem to know more than you plausibly could, or you'll give us away. Ah—my good Anaxagoras, it is the greatest

pleasure to have helped a so distinguished savant
as yourself—but I think I hear our host.''

Meton beckoned them toward the door at the
farther end of the court. Through this door they
entered a large and barely furnished room with a
floor of stone. In one far corner stood another
altar; in the other, a great pile of manuscripts,
work sheets, drawing instruments, and the like,
which litter looked as though it had been hastily
pushed aside to make room for the couches which
the slaves were now setting out.

Bulnes sighed as he resigned himself to a discomfort he had so far escaped: that of eating
gentleman-style, reclining on a sofa.

In briefing him on Athenian customs and manners, Flin had dilated on the glories of the Athenian dinner party with its contests of wit and song
and its other formidable qualities. This one, however, proved much simpler. Meton seemed to
have simply stretched his originally modest meal
of fish, bread, and assorted greens. He occupied
the head couch with Sokrates, and instead of discussing questions of ponderous philosophic import, they chattered about sports and the high cost
of living and the doings of their mutual acquaintances, while a pet marten climbed over them.

At the other side Flin, sprawled with Anaxagoras, argued the question of whether the
moon was inhabited, leaving Bulnes to munch his
celery in solitary silence. Bulnes did so, except
when Anaxagoras became involved in an argument with a slave whom he accused of serving
him wine of a grade inferior to that of the rest of
the company. Then Bulnes spoke across to Flin,

"At last, my dear Wiyem, I've found a race who cook worse than the English!"

"Huh. At least they don't smother everything with pepper the way they do in Spain. When I got back from there, I thought I should have to have a new skin grafted to the inside of my mouth."

"And the lack of women makes it seem like living in an American YMCA . . ."

"What is that?" said Meton.

Flin answered the astronomer in the latter's language, "A thousand pardons, my dear sir. We have been praising your splendid cuisine."

Meton snorted. "Nothing splendid about it. It is the Corinthians and barbarians who live for their bellies."

"Precisely," said Bulnes. "So heathfully modest in quantity and rugged in quality! None of your guests will ever stuff self till he becomes useless ball of fat."

Sokrates added sententiously, "Nothing in excess. Let us eat to live, not live to eat."

Meton shot a sharp look at Bulnes, then apparently decided to take the comment at its face value.

"Oh, well," he said, "if you put it that way, I am glad you appreciate it. However, since you have set us a task this evening, we will not waste time matching verses from the Poet or tossing dregs at a mark. As the stars will soon be out, we shall have one more pull at the wine, and then off to the roof."

Flin, catching the eye of Bulnes, flicked a thumb toward the big door that led to the rear of the house, through which the food had come,

"See that, Knut? For all we know Thalia might be back there. We have no way of finding out."

"The entrance to the seraglio, eh?"

Flin nodded. "It drives me mad when I think . . ."

They reached the roof by a ladder. Bulnes was a little alarmed to see Anaxagoras struggling up behind the rest, but the ancient bag of bones reached the top without visible difficulty.

The roof itself was flat and made of some composition like adobe. From here Bulnes could appreciate the figure-eight plan of the house, with its two open interior courts and blank outer wall. He walked over to the corner where stood a group of primitive astronomical instruments: sighting devices more or less like the forestaffs and astrolabes of later centuries, with angles marked off in simple fractions of a circle.

Meton adjusted one of the instruments.

"Come here, Bouleus," he said. "Look along these sights. Now, see you that star, the tip of the tail of the Little Bear? And that one, the brightest star in the tail of the Dragon? And that one, the nearest one to it in the constellation Cepheus? Move your pointer about one-fifth from the first star to the second, and you will be very close to the point you seek. It is unfortunate that there is no bright star near the spot . . ."

"Wiyem!" cried Bulnes in English. "It's still in its normal position!"

"What do you mean by that?"

"I mean we're still in the twenty-seventh century, *Anno Domini!* If we were back in the fifth B.C., it would be—let's see—the other side of Alpha Ursae Minoris, over towards Alpha

Draconis. If I had a good star map, I could show you exactly . . ."

"No!" cried Flin.

"Look at it yourself."

"Oh, blast it, you know I'm ignorant about such matters. But this can't all be a fake. It's too good!"

"There's your evidence. At least it makes finding Thalia a bit more hopeful."

"What are you two saying?" asked Meton.

Bulnes answered gravely in Greek, "Know, O friends, we have found Athens is a few hundred stadia north from Tartessos. If Anaxagoras will put southern tip of Greece on the same latitude as our Phaiakian city, he shall be very close to the truth."

As they walked homeward with Sokrates, Bulnes said, "Ahem—ah—Sokrates, perhaps you can help us . . ."

"In what way?"

"Like yourself, we often find that vulgar money matters interfere with the search for higher truths. To be frank, the stipend with which our city sent us forth is shrinking like the snows in spring, and—uh . . ."

"Gentlemen," said Sokrates, "were I as rich as Kallias, I should be glad to help you, but as it is . . ."

"I did not mean that. We have considered honest methods of fattening our purses before proceeding to our next stop, and it strikes us that, since some of our scientific ideas seem unknown here, perhaps we could set ourself up as professor like Protagoras . . ."

"Well?" said Sokrates in a sharper tone.

"We thought you could advise us how much to charge and where to round up some pupils . . ."

"I? I, who for years have been deploring and ridiculing the prostitution of philosophy by these same hucksters? I help you to continue this debasement of the divine faculties? My good men, you have been misinformed . . ."

"Excuse us, please," said Bulnes. "Let us consider the proposal as not having been make."

"Of course," continued Sokrates, "not being Athenians, you could not be expected to view these matters according to civilized standards of honor. I suggest you consult Protagoras himself, who is well qualified to advise you in the liming of twigs to catch some of our more credulous birds. And here our paths diverge. Rejoice!"

Off he strode, his paunch bobbing before him.

"I'm afraid he's sore at us," said Bulnes. "But what else could I have done?"

"Dash it all," said Flin. "You shouldn't have gone at him hammer-and-tongs like that. What shall we do now?"

Bulnes shrugged. "Follow his advice and ask Protagoras, I suppose."

TEN

Protagoras drew himself up to his full height (about that of Flin) and said, "My good men, you ask me to help set you up in competition with myself, and to divide with you the pupils I have attracted—or, I should say, who have at last recognized the worth of my teachings after my many years of neglect? And being, moreover, not even Hellenes, but Barbarians whose Greek I can barely understand? Are you mad? Be off with you! I have no time for lunatics."

A couple of the pupils of Protagoras, looking on, made matters even more painful by jeering.

Bulnes listened to the tirade with eyebrows raised in an expression of mild surprise. When it was over, he tossed the loose end of his himation over his shoulder and said, "Thank you, my dear Protagoras. Even if you cannot fulfill our request, you have give us free a valuable lessons in the greatness of soul to be found in Athens. Come, Philon."

And with a dignity surpassing that of Protagoras he turned his back and started off. This time the laughter was on the other side.

"Gentlemen!" said a soft voice.

A young man, who had been sitting behind one of the pillars, now spoke to Bulnes. He looked to be about thirty, with a fuzzy young beard and a nervous smile playing around his mouth.

"Something?" said Bulnes.

"Yes, if you—ah—if you really do not mind," said the young man. "I realize of course that I have no right to force myself upon you . . ."

"Come to the point, my dear sir," said Bulnes.

"Well—ah—if you will forgive me, I overheard your exchange with Protagoras—not that I would say aught against the great Protagoras—but—ah—I know not how to say it . . ."

Bulnes said, "Come, come—begin at the beginning. There are no need to be shy with us."

"That is good of you, but what I am trying to say is that if you are the Tartessian philosophers and are seriously looking for pupils, I—ah—would you consider me? I realize that you are men of importance, but then I have studied under Protagoras and Leukippos, and have spent seven years in Egypt, so you will not find me utterly unworthy of your efforts, I hope."

"Gladly," said Bulnes, masking his joy. "If you would care to come with us back to our inn, we will discuss terms and hours."

"Demokritos!" cried the voice of Protagoras behind them. "By Herakles, where have you been?

Nobody in Athens has seen you. When did you get here?"

"Oh," said the young man. "Truly, I am sorry if I have inconvenienced you, O Protagoras, but I did not wish to burst in on one of your invaluable lectures."

"But why have you not made yourself known to Sokrates or Diogenes or our other colleagues?"

Demokritos dug patterns in the dirt with the toe of his sandal. "I—I could not force myself upon them. They are godlike men of established reputation . . ."

"Nonsense! You are as wise as any, however you try to dissemble the fact. What are you doing with these Tartessians?"

"I thought—that is to say—they are offering courses and have kindly consented to enroll me."

"The hawk takes flying lessons from the chicken. Well, strangers, any time you find the Greek language too much for you and wish to share with me the money you will extract from Demokritos, I will consider brushing up your speech. After all, it is I who first classified the parts of speech and formulated the rules of grammar. Meanwhile, rejoice!"

Protagoras went back to his pupils, while Demokritos, beaming, walked away with Bulnes and Flin. The latter said, "We're going to teach Demokritos? Gah!"

"What of it, if he can pay?"

"It's like teaching Newton or Einstein! This modest lad has one of the greatest brains of all time!"

"My dear Wiyem, only last night we learned

he's not Demokritos at all, but a modern man impers—"

"Nothing of the sort! Vasil could have found some way of warping time to bring Periklean Greece forward instead of sending us back! One's no more incredible than the other."

"You're an incorrigible rationalizer, Wiyem. Personally, I've never been convinced of either. I think it's all a hoax."

"Oh, no! Not that! Perhaps—d'you know the theory of alternate time streams? We might be in another time stream which follows the same course as our own, but three thousand years later. So this world has only evolved as far as the Periklean Age, whereas our own . . ."

"Suit yourself, comrade." Bulnes turned to the Greek. "My colleague and I were discussing what sort of course to give you. Perhaps you would like lectures on Tartessian theories of the shape and motion of the earth?"

"That were most exciting!"

"Or the nature of matter?"

"Better yet!" cried Demokritos, and to the astonishment of Bulnes seized his hand and kissed it. "You gentlemen are much too kind. Perhaps it will interest you to compare your theory with that which I received from my master Leukippos, and to which I have made a few trifling additions of my own."

"What theory is that?"

"I call it the atomic theory, from the 'atoms' or tiny indivisible particles of which we suppose things to be made. It is my notion that whereas some of these atoms are smooth, so that they slide

freely past each other as in fluids, others are provided with hooks by which they become en-
tangled in fixed masses, as we see in solids . . ."

Later, when Demokritos had departed, Flin
said, "Look here, Knut, there's no sense in having
both of us hang around the inn while he's here.
One's enough for lecturing."

"You mean you'd like to handle it alone?"

"No, no, on the contrary. You lecture while I
hunt my wife."

"What? Don't be ridiculous, my friend. I can't
speak the language well enough."

"Certainly you can. You know the modern language and have an extraordinary natural aptitude.
Part of it must be that Spanish is phonetically
similar to Greek."

"Oh, come. I can ask for a loaf of bread, maybe,
but a lecture on the solar . . ."

Flin rushed on, "You're perfectly competent.
All you need is confidence, and you'll never learn
to do by yourself while I'm here to translate. We'll
run over the talk now, and everything'll be top-
hole."

"What have you in mind?" Against his better
judgment Bulnes was disarmed by the flattery of
Flin, who was usually readier with complaints
and criticisms.

"We'll rough out the first lecture this evening,
and tomorrow you'll take care of him while I
search for Thalia."

"How will you do that if all the women are
locked up?"

"It's not quite so bad as that. There are some

occasions that bring them out: religious ceremonials, of which there are a good many, and the performance of tragedies. O Podokles!"

"You wish?" said the innkeeper.

"When we left the Peiraieus, they were just about to play the Dionysiac tragedies, and they told us these plays would be shown in Athens in a few days. When is that to be?"

Podokles pondered, counting on his fingers. "Today is the seventh of Elaphebolion. . . Therefore the first one will be the day after tomorrow. By Sophokles, I am told."

"Are you going?"

"Yes, if nought befall that requires me at the inn."

"Would you like a companion?"

Podokles gave Flin one of his suspicious looks. "As a foreigner you would have to pay to get in."

"I know. Let us consider it a date, then. What happens tomorrow, if anything?"

"A special assembly of the citizens to ratify Perikles's new treaty. You cannot attend, you know."

"There you are," said Flin to Bulnes. "You lecture, I hunt. And don't feel badly about missing the play. You'd find it a weird business with those masks and stilts, anyway."

Bulnes, though he realized that he was the natural leader of the pair, felt lost without Flin when Demokritos showed up for his lecture. To one whose command of the language was still so imperfect, it was comforting to have the little man around when one got stuck.

Demokritos closed the session by saying, "Before I go, Bouleus, I—I thought perhaps you—ah—would consider another pupil?"

"Certainly. Whom?"

"Kritias Kallaischrou, the son of my host. When I applied to the proxenos having charge of visitors from Abdera, he arranged for me to stay at the house of Kallaischros."

"That sounds good."

"However—it embarrasses me to say it—there is one matter—I trust you will forgive my impertinence . . ."

Bulnes sighed. "I forgive everything in advance, if you will—uh—only come to the point."

"The family, being among the richest in Athens, would not dream of entering an inn. You would have to come to the house of Kallaischros."

"That is agreeable. Will you conduct me there tomorrow?"

Demokritos assented and departed, and then Flin came in with an odd look on his face.

"Kritias Kallaischrou?" he said when Bulnes had told him the news. "That must be the 'Kritias' of Plato's dialogues—an uncle or cousin of Plato. Brilliant, but a frightful bounder in politics. However, he'll be only a young fellow now."

"What happened to you?" said Bulnes.

"Just had an odd experience. I spoke to Perikles."

"Do tell! What happened?"

Flin chewed his lip and stared into space. "Dash it all. I knew there'd be no women at the *Ekklesia*, but I wanted to see what I could so I went over to the Pnyx. Of course, since I didn't have a citizen's pass, the Scythians wouldn't let me in, but I hung around the entrance and heard much of what went on inside. Perikles put over his treaty, though the demagogues raised a row about knuckling under to Sparta. Then the president of the session adjourned the meeting, and out they came. I picked out a good-looking, gray-haired chap in the midst of the first lot. I had a feeling I'd seen him somewhere, and wondered what he'd look like without the shrubbery on his face. The others were all talking at once and waving their hands, but not this one—very quiet and composed.

"Some other man brushed past and shouted something about his having betrayed the interests of the people, and there'd have been a jolly good row if the Scythians hadn't broken it up. But from what they said I knew the dignified chap was Perikles, and the other, a big fat individual, was Kleon the Tanner, one of his left-wing opponents.

"I took my courage in my hands and stepped up to him, saying: 'Perikles Xanthippou, may I have a word?' 'Speak,' he said. 'I'm told,' I said, 'that a group of the radical opposition are planning to attack you through your friends. They're going to trump up charges against Anaxagoras, Pheidias, and Aspasia.'

"He looked me up and down and said, 'Who are you?' 'Philon of Tartessos,' I told him. He said, 'You seem well-informed for a foreigner. Be assured that I also keep track of current affairs.' And off he went, leaving me feeling foolish. Then the rest of the crowd came pouring out and swept me along with them. It sounded like what your

American friends call the brush-off. I'd expected him to be more affable. And I still can't get over that feeling I know the man. Blast it, I begin to think you're right, that this is all a masquerade. I could cry, I'm so disappointed."

"Cheer up, my dear colleague," said Bulnes. "Suppose this were the real Periklean Athens. Then, even if you found your Thalia, what could you do then? How could you get back to your own time? Assuming you wish to, of course."

"You may assume," said Flin gloomily. "I've seen enough of Periklean Athens in the raw to last me some time. I say, you haven't a cig— There, see what I mean?"

The house of Kallaischros proved larger and better appointed than that of Meton, though laid out on the same general plan. Demokritos said to Bulnes, "This is your new pupil, Kritias, and this is my host, the noble Kallaischros."

"Rejoice!" said Bulnes. "This are—is—a great pleasure."

"How like you our violet-crowned city?" said Kallaischros.

"Magnificent!" said Bulnes. "Its institutions, also, I find most advanced and interesting. Perhaps we could—uh—apply some of them to advantage with Tartessos."

Kallaischros snorted. "Not if you know what is good for you. Democracy! Pah!"

"The regime of Perikles, then, does not meet with universal approval?"

"That man in the Odeion!" shouted Kallaischros. "Why anyone reared in one of our best families with every advantage should turn traitor to his class in order to curry popularity with the base ignorant rabble . . ."

"Do not get excited, Father," said Kritias, a fuzzy-faced youth with a pet monkey on his shoulder. "It is bad for you."

". . . to experiment with our sacred constitution, to waste the Delian treasury on an extravagant program of unnecessary public works . . ."

"Father!"

Bulnes said, "But, sir, I should think that you, as a Eupatrid, would approve this new agreement with Sparta."

"The treaty I approve, but without condonation of its author. If Perikles thinks he can crawl back into the good graces of the better sort of people by a last-minute repentance . . ."

"Father!"

"You are right, son. I should not even think of politics, this vulgar demagogy makes me so furious. It was not like this when I was young . . . But to your lessons."

Bulnes found the way wearing. While Demokritos, though brilliant, was a docile, modest, and sweet-tempered pupil, Kritias proved a scholar of a different sort—a bumptious, argumentative, sharp-tongued youth who took delight in embarrassing his teacher. When Bulnes fell afoul of the complexities of Classical Greek, Kritias would solemnly tell his monkey, "He mixes his case endings just like a milk-drinking barbarian, does he not?"

And the monkey would wag its little head in a Greek affirmative.

By noon, when the lecture ended, Bulnes was glad to get back to the inn of Podokles to sprawl on a bench and drink a pint of wine with his lunch. He was feeling slightly drunk when a shabby youth came in. Bulnes thought he looked familiar, but could not place him until the newcomer, approaching, said, "My master sends me . . ."

"Oh, you are Dromon, the slave of Sokrates?"

"That is right. Sokrates sends me to tell you that your friend, the other Tartessian, is in the House."

"In what house?"

"In the desmoterion, of course."

"What is that?"

Dromon sighed his exasperation. "A place where evil-doers are kept before they are tried."

"In jail?" Bulnes jumped up. "In the name of Zeus, why?"

"I do not know. He made some disturbance at the play, and the Scythians carried him off."

ELEVEN

The "House" stood at the north end of the
Agora—a small, nondescript brick building
whose rooms opened outward. In one of these
stinking cells sat Wiyem Flin, shackled to a ring
in the wall by a fetter on one ankle.

"So there you are!" he cried. "Where the devil
have you been? I've sat here for hours and I'm
jolly well starved."

"I'm sorry," said Bulnes. "I came as soon as I
heard." His jaw muscles tightened.

"Well, why didn't you start hunting when I
didn't come back from the play on time? And why
haven't you brought some lunch?"

"Don't they feed you here?"

"Of course not. Any ass knows that. Why didn't
you . . ."

"My dear sir," said Bulnes, eyeing the little

man coldly. "I've done the best I could, and if you're going to be a farstard, I'll simply go away until you stop."

Flin mumbled something apologetic. Bulnes asked the prisoner, "What happened this time?"

"It wasn't really my fault. You'd have done the same if you weren't such a cold-blooded . . ."

"Get to the point, please."

"Blast it, I'm trying to tell you! I went to the performance of *Aias* with Podokles and saw Thalia in the women's section, as I thought I might."

"You did!"

"Yes, I did. There was no mistake."

"Are you sure it was the right woman?"

"I ought to know my own wife after being married for eleven years! When the play was over, I hurried to the exit and stopped Thalia on her way out. 'Thalia!' I said. 'I'm here!' She looked at me blankly and replied, in Greek, that she didn't understand—'*Ouk' oída.*' So I repeated what I'd said in that language.

"She said, 'You've made a mistake. My name isn't Thalia.' 'Oh, yes it is,' I said. 'I'm Melite, the wife of Euripides Mnesarchou,' she said. 'Go away and stop bothering me.' And she started to brush past me.

"I lost my head a bit, I suppose, and caught her wrist, saying, 'Thalia, don't you know your own husband?' Then she screamed for help, and the next thing I knew a couple of the Scythians had grasped my arms and hauled me out under the direction of a tall chap with a tremendous long beard. This, it turned out, was Euripides himself, the great playwright.

"One thing about a small town like this, it doesn't take you long to get from place to place. It can't have been ten minutes before those coppers had marched me all the way from the theater around the Akropolis to the Agora, where the Polemarchos holds forth. We had to wait at the Epiloukeion for the Polemarchos to show up, because he'd been at the play like the other citizens. When he did come, Euripides laid a complaint before him of second-degree assault or something of the sort. The Polemarchos asked me if I had anything to say, and I was so rattled by that time I could only babble about Thalia's being my wife and not that of Euripides. Which made no impression. So the Polemarchos ordered me confined under a bail of five mnai pending my trial. What are you going to do about it?"

A tart sentence formed in Bulnes's mind, asking Flin why he should do anything for a damned fool, but with his usual self-control the Spaniard thought better of saying it aloud.

"Five mnai, eh? That's five hundred drachmai, which would be about—ah—seventy-five to a hundred krauns in modern money. Not unreasonable, I suppose, but much more than I have."

"Why not ask one of your pupils? Demokritos seems pretty well upholstered, and Kritias is simply rolling in the stuff."

"An idea, comrade. Definitely an idea."

"How'd you find out about me?" asked Flin.

"Sokrates sent his slave to tell me."

"He did? Dashed decent, considering how vexed he was with us. That's the real Sokrates for you."

"Yes?" said Bulnes, cocking a skeptical eyebrow. "We shall see about that. Meanwhile, I'll get you some lunch and then go see about raising bail."

"Hurry up about it," said Flin. "If I'm knocked on the head and thrown into the Barathron, it'll be all your fault. And none of that beastly barley porridge, mind you!"

Bulnes, wondering what he had done to deserve so unreasonable a companion, departed rather than argue the point. In the Agora he bought a loaf of bread, a bunch of mixed vegetables, and a cheap cup and plate to hold the victuals. He filled the cup at a public fountain and carried the meal back to Flin, who sneered at it but fell ravenously to eating.

Bulnes then hiked to the house of Kallaischros and asked for Demokritos. As neither Kallaischros nor Kritias nor Demokritos was in, the porter told Bulnes, "The young men have gone to the Kynosarges. Kritias usually attends the Akademeia, but they have gone to the other gymnasium because Demokritos is not a citizen."

Bulnes set out again. He found the street that ran over the low saddle between the Areopagos and the Akropolis and toiled over it into the south part of town, which he had not previously visited. He would have gotten hopelessly lost in the tangle of narrow streets except that he kept looking back at the Akropolis to orient himself. Outside the Diomean Gate, near the great unfinished Olympieion, lay the Kynosarges, a small park.

The Scythian at the entrance looked Bulnes over to see that he bore no slave brands and waved him on in. Bulnes passed a couple of altars and came to a large quadrangle comprising a gym building and a series of porticoes.

In and around the quadrangle naked men were running, jumping, wrestling, and otherwise exerting themselves. Bulnes (who took a dim view of calisthenics) passed them by, for they reminded him that he possessed the beginnings of a middle-aged paunch, which he somehow never found time, energy, or will power to train back. At length he located Demokritos in a huddle under one of the porticoes. The young man was engaged in a game of Greek checkers, with several kibitzers standing around.

Demokritos looked up and said, "Rejoice, my dear Bouleus! I shall be through here directly, as soon as I have forced this man's stones off the sacred line."

He made a move, and his opponent said, "That does it. Away with you, man of Abdera! Tyche is too good to you."

As the group broke up a voice said, "The Tartessian professor! What can we do for you here?" It was Kritias, with dirt on his face and his skin glistening with oil. "How would three falls out of five suit you? Come now . . ."

"If you please, gentlemen," said Bulnes, "I am here on more serious business. My colleague are in prison."

Kritias laughed loudly. "That is good! What has he done, broken into the treasure of Athene Parthenos? Tried to pass himself off as a citizen in hope of snaring a juror's pay?"

"Not so serious as that, but vexatious, nevertheless."

He thereupon began the story he had been rehearsing.

"When we dwelt in Tartessos, my colleague Philon had a wife on whom he doted. But on an evil day a Carthaginian galley raided the coast near our city for slaves and caught my poor friend's wife. Ever since then he has been a little mad on this one subject. When he sees a woman he think looks like his wife, he will have it that it is indeed she and tries to claim her."

"And he has been claiming the wife of one of our people?" said Kritias.

"Exactly so. It was at the play this morning, and the victim was the wife of Euripides the playwright, who had my friend thrown in jail for making a disturbance."

"That will teach him," said Kritias.

Demokritos said, "On the contrary, it proves my point, my dear Kritias. You will remember my saying that in an ideal commonwealth, slavery would not be allowed."

"Nonsense!" said Kritias. "Without slaves, who would do the work? We, of course, and we should therefore have no time for sports, art, science, and literature. In other words, no slaves, no civilization."

"But there ought to be . . ." began Demokritos.

"Besides," continued Kritias, "it is logical that

we Hellenes, who alone of the peoples of the world combine valor with intelligence, should rule the stupid northerners and the cowardly southerners. However, I will concede that in an individual case, like that of our Tartessian friend, the seizing of a person seems an undeserved hardship. But what is to be done?"

Bulnes said, "First, he is in jail on bail of five mnai, which I do not have."

Demokritos and Kritias looked at one another. The former said, "I am sorry, but when I planned this trip to Athens, I did not allow for such an unexpected expense. However, it is otherwise with you, O Kritias."

"We do not after all know these Tartessians very well."

"Oh, I think we can trust Bouleus. He stands to gain more from his lecture course than by letting his friend jump bail."

"Fair enough," said Kritias. "If you will remind me when you appear for the lecture tomorrow, Bouleus, the money shall be given you."

Bulnes said, "Thanks you, my dear friends. However, while I dislike exceedingly to seem ungrateful, my poor colleague am still in the House with a fetter on his leg, and there he will stay until bailed. You have not the sum with you, have you?"

"My dear man," said Kritias, "I do not carry the family patrimony on my back as an invitation to every footpad in Athens. And as I do not wish to leave my exercise here, you will have to wait till tomorrow."

"I see," said Bulnes. "Perhaps you could advise

me what to do next, as I am not familiar with your laws?"

Kritias said, "Your best chance, I should say, would be to persuade the complainant to withdraw his complaint. Said you he was Euripides the poet?"

"Yes. Where is he to be found?"

"He has a house in the Peiraieus, but most of his time he spends on Salamis. The man is said to be a worse recluse than Timon. Rejoice!" And Kritias strolled off, singing:

"My wealth is a sword and my fortune a spear
  And a buckler of rawhide I carry before me.
 I plow and I sow and I reap with this gear,
 I press the sweet vintage and make serfs adore
    me."

The sun had sunk low when Bulnes knocked on the door of the house of Euripides in Peiraieus. It had taken him over an hour to walk down from Athens, and another half-hour to locate the house by incessant questioning, for most streets had no names, and house numbers had not even been thought of. He had put aside the temptation to wander down to the waterfront to look at the boats and ships, for, as a yachting enthusiast, he was much more interested in these objects than in many-columned Greek temples.

Bulnes resolved, if he ever got out of this alive, to spend a month on the *Dagmar II* just drifting and never walking more than five steps at a time.

If he continued to dwell in Periklean Athens, perhaps he could someday procure a horse—or no, that would not do. A burro or a mule would more likely be within his means. Moreover, never having ridden an animal of any sort, he did not care, in a stirrupless age, to begin his riding career quite so far from the ground as the back of a horse.

He also worried about Flin, who would have kittens if he did not get a progress report. However, Bulnes could not spend half his time trotting back to the Oikema. Perhaps, as Kritias in his crude way had implied, a night in the *calabozo* would do the little man good.

The spy hole opened. "No, the master is not in."

"When do you expect him?"

"I do not know. Who are you?"

"Bouleus of Tartessos."

"What do you want?"

"I should like to discuss the regrettable incident of this morning at the Dionysia."

"You mean when the barbarian tried to kidnap the mistress?"

"Yes," said Bouleus.

"You will have to come back later."

Bulnes said, "Look, I have just walked down from Athens. May I at least come in to rest for a few minutes?"

"No, I cannot admit anybody in the master's absence. Go away!"

Bulnes was about to stagger off when he heard voices raised in argument. Then the same slave's face appeared again at the hole. "The mistress says you may come in."

Que esta? thought Bulnes. Much as he wanted a

place to rest, people who invaded one of these
quasi-Oriental harems in the absence of the
sheikh were likely to regret it. On the other hand,
so tired and footsore was he that if the Devil had
thrown open the door to Hell and asked him in, he
would have taken him up on it.

The mistress of the house awaited him in the
andronitis. Bulnes looked hard at her as he came
forward. It was Thalia, all right, perfectly recognizable despite her long chiton and the silver tiara
on her glossy-black hair—a woman in her mid-
thirties, still attractive in a lush, full-blown way.
Although he had not disliked Flin's wife, back in
England, he had never taken much to her, either.
She was quite intelligent, but a garrulous and
gossippy female, and definitely the dominating
half of the couple. However, a childish personality like that of Wiyem Flin no doubt needed
domination.

He looked her in the eye for any spark of recog-
nition, but saw none. Instead, she gave him the
hand wave, with the back of the hand outwards,
that here took the place of a handshake. She said,
"Rejoice, good Bouleus. Euripides will be home
in an hour or so, and meanwhile there is no point
in your wandering the Peiraieus like the ghost of
an unburied corpse. Sosias, fetch a stool for the
gentleman and a small stoup of wine. (See his
frown—he thinks your presence here will com-
promise me.) And rout out Euages to take the ferry
over to Salamis and tell the master he has a vis-
itor." She turned back to Bulnes. "I understand
you have come on behalf of the other Tartessian,
he who accosted me this morning?"

"Yes," said Bulnes, sitting down gratefully.

"Whatever possesseth man to act so? Tell me—
I am all agog to know. Is he mad? Is he in rut and
cannot wait a few days for the Aphrodisia?"

"The first guess were nearly right, madam,"
said Bulnes, and told Thalia-Melite the same tale
he had told his pupils.

"The poor fellow," she said. "I am sure that
under this circumstance Euripides will withdraw
the complaint. My husband has a good heart if
you can get him down from the clouds long
enough."

"I am told," said Bulnes, "that Euripides
spends most of his time on Salamis?"

"Yes, the old dotard! Every morning before
dawn he and Kephisophon take their boat across
the channel, with one of the slaves to row, and
there they spend the day scribbling. He claims he
cannot concentrate in a house full of wives and
children and slaves, which is ridiculous. As if his
wretched plays were more important than his
own household!"

"Who is Kephisophon?"

"His secretary. The Euripides is becoming one
of the standard sights of Athens, along with the
Akropolis and the ship of the divine Theseus. I am
told that guides harangue visitors about him:
'And there, gentlemen, is the island of Salamis,
scene of the great sea fight against the trousered
Mede, and there is the cave of the eminent poet
Euripides. If you row out a few furlongs, you can
see Euripides himself in the entrance, no doubt
working on some sublime new drama.' And if I
complain of neglect he says, 'I am really doing it

all for you, my dear,' which does not deceive me in the least.''

"A man thoroughly absorbed in his work?" said Bulnes.

"Absorbed! Why, he will not take the time to buy food for the house, which every man in Athens does as a matter of course, so the slaves swindle us right and left. Personally, I think little of these Attic customs, but must not one conform to some degree?''

"You are not an Athenian?''

"Yes and no. My parents were, so I rank as a citizen, but my father was ostracized and spent his exile in hollow Lakedaimon, where I was reared. There women are personalities in their own right and not playthings locked in a chest when not in use.''

"You must find it quite a contrast.''

"Contrast!'' she leaned forward on her stool. "Many a time I have thought I should go mad. Why think you I told them to admit you? Danae in her tower had no more frustrating lot, locked up with no company but a husband old enough to be my father, and occasional visits from these vapid Athenian dames—I, who as a young girl ran and wrestled naked on the athletic field like a man . . .''

During this conversation she had been hitching her stool farther and farther forward, and now was gently pressing her thigh against his. Her face was flushed, breath coming fast, dark eyes half-closed and mouth half open. All the slaves seemed to have vanished.

Bulnes's own pulse began to pound—but then

he thought of the enormous complications and decided to be good—this once anyway. Another time . . .

He drew back stiffly, saying, "Tell me, what is Euripides working on now? For rumors of his fame have reached far Tartessos."

"Oh," she said, with a look that expressed regret for having admitted this stick of a foreigner in the first place. "Some huge tetralogy—I never keep track of his works . . ."

TWELVE

The street door opened. In came a man as tall as
Bulnes, with bushy eyebrows, a patriarchal nose,
and a graying beard down to his solar plexus.
Behind him a younger man with a mass of
papyrus-rolls under his arm looked askance at
Bulnes, though the older one seemed to find
nothing amiss.

"Bouleus of Tartessos? Bouleus of Tartessos?
Do I know you, my dear fellow? Thank you, Melite, but you had better go back into the
gynaikonitis like a good girl. What said you your
name was, my dear sir?"

Bulnes told him again.

"Ah, yes, I remember. Why you scoundrel, you
are the barbarian who caused such an unseemly
disturbance this mor— But no, that cannot be,
because you are tall and thin like me, whereas this

man was short and thick like Kephisophon. Was
he not from Tartessos too? Do you know him?"

Bulnes told his prepared story.

"Ah, yes, that is the way of it. It shows the
inscrutable workings of Fate, for if Melite had not
had a cold last week, she would have seen the
Aias at the local theater, and I should not have had
to convey her all the way to Athens. How did you
hear of this regrettable incident?"

"Our friend Sokrates sent his slave to inform
me."

"Do you mean Sokrates Sophroniskou the
philosopher?"

"Yes."

"Why said you not so at once? Sokrates is an old
and valued friend of mine, and any friend of his is
welcome. What did you think of the play?"

"I have not see it," said Bulnes.

"Oh . . . you are not the man who attended it
and accosted my wife. What say you his name is?
Philon of Tartessos. Ah, yes. A wonderful trage-
dian, the Sophokles, think you not? We are
friendly rivals, you know. He was good enough to
say that without my competition this year it is like
no contest at all."

"Why are you not competing?"

"I did not finish my tetralogy in time. I am so
wretchedly absent-minded, I forgot that the date
comes early this year."

"Really?" said Bulnes, glad to remember some
of the lectures on Greek drama Wiyem Flin had
inflicted upon him. "Is one of the plays about the
witch Medeia?"

"Why, yes. How could you know?"

"It seemed likely. I know the general plot of that myth. It has penetrated even to Tartessos, as has your own poetic reputation."

"Yes, you are quite a literate and civilized people, are you not? I hope to work in a good word in the *Medeia* for regarding barbarians as fellow human beings. Could I read you some of the passages we worked out today?"

"I should be honored."

"Very well, Kephisophon, find that section where Iason offers Medeia to provide for her after their divorce. . . . Ah, here we are."

And the dramatist began tramping back and forth in the court, orating, waving his manuscript, and flapping his himation:

"Oh, peace! Enough
Of these vain wars: I will no more thereof.
If thou wilt take of all that I possess
Aid for these babes and thine own helplessness
Of exile, speak thy bidding. Here I stand
Full-willed to succor them . . ."

His incredible beard lashed the spring air. Every few minutes he would turn on Bulnes with, "How do you like that?"

Bulnes made comments as intelligent as his limited knowledge permitted, and even suggested a trifling change or two. Then a slave came out of the gynaeceum and whispered into the ear of Euripides.

"Ah, I forgot again! Hippodamos is coming for dinner!" said the poet. "My dear fellow, I hate to rush you off this way, but you know how it is.

Here, take a piece of manuscript with you to read.
I should like your criticism, since you seem well-
informed in such matters. Kephisophon, find the
rough draft of the opening scene and give it to
Bouleus. You understand, though, Bouleus, that
the final version is considerably improved."

"Thank you," said Bulnes. "But excuse
me . . ."

"Oh, yes, there was something else you wished
to see me about. Now what was it?"

"About my friend in the jail. Will you withdraw
the complaint?"

"Certainly, now that you have explained it.
What was your explanation? No matter. Let me
see—I shall not go to Athens soon again, but I will
write a letter tomorrow and send it to the
Polemarchos by a slave. Remind me of that,
Kephisophon. And now rejoice, my foreign
friend, and fail not to let me know your opinion of
the play."

Bulnes stepped out into the broad street and
started back toward Athens. His rest had much
strengthened him, and now if he could only get a
bite to eat . . . He stopped as he passed the Hip-
podamian Agora and bought a small loaf and a
sausage (to hell with trichinosis, he thought) and
a scoop of mustard. With these he made a fair
approximation of an American hot dog, a snack he
had grown very fond of in that country.

He resumed his hike, holding his loaf with one
hand and munching, and the roll of manuscript
with the other. The sausage seemed to be made
mainly of blood and tripe, not bad but not very
tasty either. He shook out the scroll and held it up

to read by the pink light of the setting sun. Hell, he thought, all the words run together. As if Greek weren't hard enough to read with the words separated! Still he'd no doubt have to make a stab at it to keep on good terms with Euripides . . .

He rolled the manuscript up, tucked it under his arm, and set off again, when a man stepped out from behind a building, snatched the scroll out from under Bulnes's arm, and ran.

"Hey!" roared Bulnes. "Come back here!"

He realized that in his excitement he had spoken English, which from many years of use had become more natural to him even than Spanish. Furthermore, he had no idea of the Greek for 'Stop thief!''

He looked around. Not a Scythian in sight. licemen were the same in all places and ages. H ran after the thief, who doubled around a couple of corners and almost lost his pursuer.

The man's chiton bobbed ahead in the twilight, heading for one of the gates. He flew through, and Bulnes pounded after him, sandals slapping. Bulnes's first thought had been of Phaleas the gangster and his band, but it did not seem likely that a member of a Peiraic gang would flee toward Athens with his loot.

Although Bulnes was hardly in shape for a five-mile run, his fury at the farstard's impertinence kept him going. Moreover, he would have an embarrassing time explaining the disappearance of the manuscript.

The thief was evidently a younger man, for he pulled steadily ahead of Bulnes on the road for Athens. He splashed through the ford across the

Kephisos, half-fell, recovered, and limped when he came out of the water on the far side. Evidently he had sprained an ankle. Bulnes regretted it wasn't his neck.

The chase continued, both walking. When Bulnes's greater length of leg brought him closer to the thief, the latter broke into a limping run and widened the distance again. Thus they hobbled, jogged, and panted toward Athens. Little by little, despite the other man's sprints, Bulnes pulled up on him. The fellow's ankle must be half killing him, Bulnes gloated.

The stars came out, and jackals yapped across the Attic plain, and still the chase continued.

The thief reached the Peiraic Gate of Athens about fifty meters ahead of Bulnes, whose hope that the guards would stop the man were again disappointed.

But they did stop Bulnes. "What you doing?" said a couple in pidgin Greek. "Gate closed for night."

"I am chasing that thief! Come along with me!"

"No thief. Who you? Maybe you thief, huh?"

Either they were determined to be stupid, or were in league with the thief. Bulnes noted that one of them had left his unstrung bow leaning against the wall.

Bulnes snatched up the bowstave. *Whonk! Whonk!* went the wood against the pointed Scythian caps. One archer sat down, the other fell forward to hands and knees.

Bulnes raced out the other end of the enclosure, his tired feet speeded by the uproar behind him. Soon Scythian boots sounded on the dirt.

As he did not think he could outrun the entire
Athenian police force, Bulnes slipped around the
first corner, threw away the bowstave, rearranged
his himation, and started back the way he had
come, toward the Peiraic Gate, like any other
stroller out for a turn in the evening. A group of
Scythians went past, asking each other loudly
which way the scoundrel had gone. Bulnes let
them bump him up against the side of the house,
made a vague gesture in response to their questions, and watched them scatter around corners
and disappear.

Meantime he had lost track of his quarry. Small
though the town might be, it was quite big enough
to hide one man in its crooked stinking alleys
beyond the possibility of digging him out—
especially at night.

Bulnes wrote off the manuscript as lost and set
out wearily for the Agora. He would have to get
another meal for Flin before turning in for the
night.

He had gone but a few blocks when he spied a
man sitting by the side of the street in the dirt,
ahead of him, with his back against the stucco
house wall and exhaustion writ in every line of
his posture. As Bulnes came in sight, however,
the man heaved himself to his feet, pushed the
hair out of his eyes, and started walking ahead of
Bulnes, also toward the Agora. He limped and
carried a roll of papyrus.

Although it was now too dark to recognize faces
at that distance, Bulnes felt sure this was his
thief. This time, however, instead of rushing upon
the man, he thought it wiser to tail him. There

must be some peculiar reason for the man's snatching the roll; it was not the booty the average thief would go for.

The man continued steadily southeast, skirting the Agora, where the wicker kiosks had all been folded up for the night. As the man reached the south end of the Agora he bore left, toward the east end of the Akropolis, which towered against the stars in front of Bulnes.

Presently the man came to a small enclosure, a kind of one-block park. Bulnes remembered the day Flin had dragged him all over the Akropolis. The little teacher had pointed out this enclosure as the Theseion, or shrine of Theseus, the leading legendary hero of the city of Athens. He would have dragged Bulnes through it, too, if the latter had not pleaded weariness.

The Theseion had a thick hedge around it. The thief hobbled along this for a way, then ducked through a hole in the shrubbery. Bulnes followed in time to see him disappearing into a small building among the trees and statues. This edifice was the shrine of Theseus: a squarish structure open at one side, a row of columns across the entrance. Bulnes ran on tiptoe to the entrance and peered around the building wall into the interior.

Inside he could dimly make out murals on the walls, an altar, and a primitive-looking cult statue on a pedestal. The thief was standing with his back to him, watching the ground behind the altar.

With a *whirr* of machinery the altar began to tilt forward. A line of light appeared along its base. The altar seemed to be fastened to the top of a trap door that was now opening. It nodded forward until it almost touched the ground, and the trap door was vertical.

The thief stepped into the opening and started down a flight of steps. One—two—three—only his upper half was in sight; then only his head; then nothing. The altar began to rise toward its former vertical position.

Bulnes rushed over to the trap door. He caught a glimpse of movement and a snatch of speech. He was sure the place below was electrically lighted, but by lamps so shaded that he could see but little. The altar rose, the lighted area contracting to a wedge.

Bulnes thought desperately of sticking his foot in the trap door; but if the door were power-operated, the result might be hard on the foot. Then, just before the light disappeared, he snatched out his sheath knife and thrust the hilt between the closing trap door and its frame. The movement stopped with a jar, leaving the altar of Theseus leaning at a slight angle.

Bulnes reflected that there was probably some code of raps or words by which the thief—a pretty well-connected sort of thief, too—announced his presence.

He put his ear to the crack. Voices still came from below. He thought the language was English spoken in a variety of accents.

Bulnes put his shoulder against the altar and pushed. To his surprise it gave. Not readily, but a centimeter at a time. Meanwhile small mechanical sounds came from beneath his feet and the machinery was forced to run in reverse. But the

minute he let go, the altar started to tip back upright again.

He put his full strength into it. Down went the
altar, slowly, with a creak and a whirr. Up from
the depths came the voices of two men: ". . . 'ow
the bloody 'ell was I to know?"

"Can you not the instructions remember?"

"They didn't cover this case."

"The sector super vill hell raise."

"But 'e was the blighter oo told me to get that
bleeding manuscript at all costs. It seems they
want to compare . . ."

Bulnes took a quick look. One of the men was
standing at the base of the steps with his back to
Bulnes. The gods were really too kind this time;
the shouting of the disputants had drowned out
the sound of the opening of the trap door.

In a swift movement Bulnes threw off his himation, picked up his knife from the ground beside
the hatch frame, and leaped for the back of the
nearer man.

THIRTEEN

As his feet struck the man's back, Knut Bulnes brought his right fist down on the fellow's head in a hammer blow. The bulge at the base of the hilt of his knife hit the man's close-cut hair, and the man collapsed.

Bulnes sprang away as the body fell forward and rolled on its side. He lit lightly on the concrete floor, having just time to observe that, whereas the small thief was dressed in an Ionic chiton (essentially a big flour-sack with holes for arms and head), the man he had just felled wore a blue-denim shirt to which was pinned a large identification badge with photograph, and a pair of work pants held up by a belt with loops through which were thrust screw drivers and similar tools.

The other man, however, more urgently claimed his attention, for he dropped a similar badge, which he had been in the act of pinning to his garment, and pulled out a knife that had been strapped to his thigh under the skirt of his chiton.

Bulnes's instincts warned him not to admit that he was anything other than one more pseudo-Periklean Hellene intent upon getting his stolen property back. Accordingly he said, in Classical Greek, "Give me that, you thief!"

At the same time he advanced, knife ready.

The little man moved, not toward Bulnes, but at an angle, toward the corner in which the blond man had been sitting. In this nook there was an office chair, a shelf on which lay a clipboard with sheets of paper attached, and a small litter of pencils, paper clips, etc. Above the shelf, on the wall, was a panel with a telephone mouthpiece and many buttons and switches.

The thief limped toward the corner, menacing Bulnes with the dagger. Bulnes guessed that he meant to push an alarm button, and with a feline leap he sprang in front of the panel.

The thief, however, came right at Bulnes, the dagger held stiffly in front of him like a fencer's foil. Bulnes knocked the man's forearm aside; his opponent, coming on headlong, impaled himself on Bulnes's own knife.

The impetus of the man's lunge drove Bulnes's arm back. Bulnes shoved hard and thrust the man backward. The thief fell supine, eyes staring upward.

Now, thought Bulnes, *I'm in for it.*

A quick check showed the small man dead and the large one likely to regain consciousness at any time. Bulnes scooped up the papyrus roll and

started up the steps down which he had come . . .
to realize that the trap door was again closed.

He placed a hand against its underside and
pushed. No result. Harder—still none. He remembered that it had taken all his strength,
applied with much greater leverage to the top of
the altar, to open it before. It probably had an
automatic locking mechanism.

He came back down the steps and examined the
panel over the shelf in the corner. There was one
big red button labeled "Djen. El." (General
Alarm), several smaller ones bearing such cryptic
abbreviations as "Kor." and "Tra," and others
identified by numbers or letters alone. There was
no way to tell, without instruction, which buttons
worked the trap door.

Bulnes looked up and down the tunnel. For the
most part it was lined with bare concrete, sloping
slightly up in one direction and down in the
other. Across the tunnel from the seat stood a
full-length mirror, and next to it a branch tunnel
went off in the direction of the Peiraieus. In the
down direction, a few meters away, an object
stood in a niche in the wall. As he walked toward
it Bulnes saw that it was a large rack for holding
six light machine guns. The guns stood like a row
of the Emperor's guards, butt plates in slots at the
bottom and muzzles projecting up through holes
in the top. The guns were secured by a steel bar
that ran horizontally through their trigger guards.
At one end, the bar projected through a hole in the
side of the rack, and at the other it entered a lock. It
was firmly fixed in place.

However, perhaps something could be done

with the rack as a whole. When he heaved on it, it leaned slightly. Though heavy, it was not immovable. By repeated tugging he hauled it out from the wall, though not so far as to clear its ends from the niche. Then he went back to his bodies.

First he appropriated the dead man's identification badge. (People seldom compared the photograph on such a badge with the face of the wearer.) Then he removed the chiton from the body of the thief and cut it into strips. With these he gagged the other man and bound his wrists and ankles. Bulnes dragged the fellow (who showed signs of reviving until quieted by another tap with the knife pommel) down the tunnel, heaved him to shoulder height with straining muscles (the man was as heavy as he), and pushed him over the top of the gun rack. The man's body fell with a multiple thump to the floor behind the rack.

Then Bulnes went back, picked up the naked corpse of the thief, and shoved it after his first victim. There was not much room between the rack and the wall behind, and Bulnes had to reach over the top of the rack and wrestle with the corpse to make it lie down out of sight and not leave a pallid foot sticking up like a mute plea for help.

Panting, he looked again about him. So long as he was stuck underground he might as well explore a little and learn as much as he could in the course of looking for another outlet. For this was evidently where they had their lair.

He again picked up the manuscript of Euripides and started down the tunnel. Beyond the gun rack the tunnel bent slightly, and around the bend he came upon another alcove in which stood two shiny motor scooters. Bulnes was tempted to try to ride one, but their master-switches proved to be locked. Presently he came to an intersection or fork. The small metal directional signs set in the wall bore legends in code: "A-64" and the like.

As he walked he became aware of a faint distant hum. The tunnel did a dog-leg. Before Bulnes knew it, he was upon another trap-door exit like that through which he had entered. At the base of the steps was a brown-skinned fellow with straight black hair, perhaps a southern Asiatic. He sat at his panel reading a magazine. The man looked up; their eyes met.

Bulnes cursed himself for hesitating. He should have breezed on by. Now, however, his pause required explanation. He thought fast, then said in his most American English, "Say, Mac, I'm a little turned around. Which way is the sector super's office?"

The title he remembered from the conversation between the thief and the other guardian of the gate. The man addressed spoke with a Hindustani accent, "Farst right, second left. It is just bepore you come to the entrance to the condeetioner substation."

"Thanks, bud," said Bulnes, and strode off.

Soon he came to another intersection. As he stepped out into it he had to jump back to avoid being run down by another man on a motor scooter. The man wore the sandals, felt hat, and chlamys or riding cloak of an Athenian ephebos. The cloak streamed out behind him leaving his body otherwise naked, as he purred past.

Remembering his instructions, Bulnes took the right-hand tunnel. The mechanical hum grew louder. More men passed him, some in the dress of Periklean Greece, others in modern working clothes. Bulnes turned left at the next intersection. More men, more scooters, more noise, more cryptic signs. Doors began to appear in the walls of the tunnel. Bulnes noted the legends on them: "9-E-401," "Fai. Dip.," and at last: SEKTER SIUP.

Bulnes toyed with the idea of walking in and handing his papyrus to the receptionist or secretary or the superintendent himself, whoever seemed prepared to receive it. He immediately vetoed the notion; first, because he might yet want to return the document to Euripides; secondly, because there was too much chance that somebody in the office might know the late thief by sight.

Hence, after a slight pause, Knut Bulnes hurried on. More noise, more people, and then an open door with a chain across it, through which most of the noise seemed to come.

The sound was a mechanical clicking and buzzing such as one heard in a large telephone exchange, and the sight glimpsed through the opening was, in fact, much like such a place. There were endless banks of gadgets, each bank reaching to the high ceiling. Relays clicked; lights flashed; and in the electro-mechanical jungle a few technicians moved casually, pressing a button or throwing a switch or simply staring at little flashing lights.

Bulnes, not wishing to attract attention by interest in a sight that must be old hat to those who worked here, walked on past the open door. He went past another like it and then turned and retraced his steps, taking a good long look through each opening.

A picture began to form in his mind. The scientists of Emperor Vasil's staff must have developed a machine that conditioned people (hence the name "conditioner") to believe any predetermined story about who they were, and when and where they had lived all their lives. Then the Emp had restored Greece to its Periklean condition (having first dismantled and stored all the genuine relics of antiquity in that country) and likewise converted some millions of Greeks into believing they were truly Sokrates, Perikles, et cetera. He had chosen his types with care, so that the pseudo-Sokrates was to all intents and purposes a replica of the real one—the right age, mentality, personality, appearance, and so on.

Vasil would have indoctrinated these unwitting actors (by some sort of super-post-hypnotic suggestion?) to correspond with all the known historical characters of the time in question: the 530's before Christ. He would moreover have indoctrinated enough others to give a lifelike human environment—the right proportions of slaves and free men, workers and aristocrats, and so forth—for the re-enactment of the drama of the Greek Golden Age. And no doubt the machine which he had glimpsed at one substation kept control of these people so that they should continue to act as they would have in the real Hellas.

The tunnel system, which might well extend all over Greece, served to maintain contact between the actors on the surface above and the unseen puppet-masters below, who could emerge by one of the secret entrances when expedient, pass among the pseudo-Athenians as one of them, gather data, and return.

That was no doubt the reason for the theft of the manuscript of Euripides. It was a datum. Why? Oh, they might want to compare the *Medeia* composed by pseudo-Euripides with the real one.

But was the machine supposed to force re-enactment of the entire history of the period? Or was Vasil simply winding the play up, as it were, and letting it go from there as the human puppets chose to play it?

In the former case, those in charge would face an impossible task. The original Periklean Greece could not be literally reproduced, because historical records existed for only a tiny fraction of its population. In most cases, even these were far too scanty to make possible an accurate re-creation of the individual. You could not hope for a lifelike synthesis of some character who was merely mentioned by Plutarch in one sentence, to say nothing of his parents, wife, children, slaves, and so on. Not to mention all the anonymous millions who had lived and died without leaving any tangible trace. Therefore, you would have to fake: imagine what so-and-so might have been like, invent a background and character for him, and hope for the best.

However, one of these historians' figments might prove a talented man who would rise in the world on his own account, or a crank who would assassinate one of the actors in the leading roles, and then what would become of Periklean history? Not to mention the ubiquitous threat of accident, how could Perikles start the Peloponnesian War if he had already died of a snake bite or been killed in a chariot wreck?

Well, *was* Periklean history going according to schedule? Bulnes decided he did not know enough Greek history to judge.

There were of course other possibilities. Perhaps Vasil IX had at his command some gadget by which he could actually snatch Periklean Hellas out of its proper space-time frame and bring it forward to this modern era, as Flin had suggested. . . . No, that wouldn't work. Bulnes was sure Euripides's wife Melite was really Flin's wife Thalia.

Or could it be that the Emp had a gadget that, while it would not disturb the real space-time fabric, would enable Vasil or his men to view what actually happened at some past time—a sort of temporal television? In this way it would be possible, by a vast enough amount of detail work, to follow the career of every real Greek of the Periklean Age from birth to death. With this mass of data one could, at least in theory, set up a pseudo-Hellas wherein every individual of the real one was approximated by some bemused modern Greek acting out his part.

But most obscure of all, why should Vasil undertake such an extraordinary enterprise?

It must be fabulously expensive. Furthermore, the Emp would be treasuring up trouble for himself by trampling on the rights of so many people—using them as guinea pigs without their

consent—in case the near-dictatorship of the Lenz
ministry should someday fall. Could it be that
Vasil was merely employing the re-enactment as
an aesthetic experience? Bulnes remembered the
stories that Vasil, a devotee of small and esoteric
cults, believed himself a reincarnation of several
great historical leaders: Perikles of Athens, Henri
Quatre of France, Franklin Roosevelt of the
United States, Kenji Nogami of Japan . . .

If this worked, would he next undertake the
re-enactment of the history of France in the six-
teenth century, or of the United States in the twentieth?

FOURTEEN

Bulnes reminded himself that the more urgent problem for him right now was to escape to the upper world again before his imposture was penetrated.

He backtracked briskly. When he arrived at the place where he had entered the tunnel system, he found a group of three people. One sat at the control panel—not the blond man with the German accent, but a dish-faced Slavic type—while two others, one in work clothes and one with a peaked cap and pistol holster that suggested a security organization, talked to him.

All three looked around as Bulnes came toward them, and he of the pistol said, "Hey, you seen Muller?"

"No," said Bulnes. "What's become of him?"

"That's what we're trying to find out. Surkov here came to relieve him, and he wasn't there. If he's wandered off to get a brew, it'll be the last of his job."

The other standing man said, "I don't think Manfred would do that. He's pretty conscientious about regs."

Bulnes felt his scalp prickle with the knowledge that Manfred Muller lay bound only a few meters away. If these employees of the System didn't locate him soon, he would probably get his gag loose and yell.

Bulnes asked the seated man, "Didn't he at least leave a note for you?"

"Not one liddle think. Nothing but dis empty sit."

"Have you checked the lavatory?" said Bulnes.

The guard said, "I got my partner doing that now."

At that instant another man appeared in the tunnel, a stout character wrapped in a himation. As he walked up, Surkov said, "Hallo, Pierre."

"Hallo yourself." Pierre unpinned his badge and laid it on the shelf below the control panel. "What is all this? A conditioned man get into the tunnels?"

"Muller has disappeared himself," said Surkov, handing Pierre the clipboard from the shelf.

Pierre signed the sheet, took a good look at himself in the full-length mirror on the opposite wall, rearranged his himation, and started to climb the stairs. Surkov reached for the control buttons.

"Hey, come back here!" said the guard. "Surkov, you never more than glanced at the picture on the badge. That man could be anybody at all."

"No, he could not. I know him. I play bezique with him." He waved the badge under the guard's nose and pushed one of the buttons. With a *whirr* of machinery the trap door began to open.

Bulnes had meant to deposit his badge and boldly walk out likewise, trusting to the human weakness that causes every security routine to become slipshod with familiarity. Now, however, that the guard was there, and since They knew something had befallen Surkov's predecessor, somebody would be sure to take a sharp look at the thief's badge adorning Bulnes's chiton, and realize that the face depicted there did not look at all like that of the man who wore it.

"Be seeing you," said Bulnes, and strolled up the slope of the main tunnel with ostentatious casualness.

Not until he had gone a good hundred meters did he dare look back. By then, the curvature of the tunnel hid the trio around the portal. The upward slope became more and more pronounced. The damned thing must surely have risen above ground level by now. Bulnes tried to orient himself but found he had completely lost track of above-ground directions. From the height, however, he guessed that the tunnel was ascending inside either the Akropolis or the Areopagos, or Mount Lykabettos.

At last the passage ended in a stair with a niche beside it where a man sat at a control board, very much like the portal through which Bulnes had entered the system. Bulnes walked boldly toward the man, unpinning his badge as he came. He laid the badge on the shelf and had his hand out for the pencil to sign the register even before the man had picked it up. He signed "Djon Hwait," laid down the pencil, and started up the stairs without a word, as if confident that the gate keeper would press the button that opened the trap.

The gate keeper reached for the control buttons, then hesitated. "Hey!" he said.

Bulnes paused to look back. "Well?"

"You forgot your key."

"Oh. Sorry." Although Bulnes did not know what the key was for, he came back down a few steps with his hand out.

The man handed him a big bronze object with a long curved prong, more like a kind of sickle than a key.

Bulnes said, "Thanks" and started back up the steps. The trap opened. Bulnes paused long enough for it to reach nearly full gape, then went up, thrusting his head into the darkness.

At that instant, an alarm bell rang loudly.

"Hey!" said the gate keeper again.

This time Bulnes kept on going.

"Come back!" said the gate keeper, reaching for a button. With a slight change in the quality of its whirr, the trap door began to close again. A glance showed Bulnes that the gate keeper was fumbling in an open drawer, no doubt for a gun.

Bulnes hurled the bronze key in his hand at the head of the gate keeper. The heavy object bounced off the man's balding cranium. As the key clattered to the floor, and the man started to fall after it, Bulnes turned. He skipped up the remaining three steps and hurled himself away from the opening. The trap door brushed his heels as he leaped out and closed with a thump and a click behind him.

Blinded by sudden darkness, Bulnes cracked his shin on some unseen object. Cursing under his breath, he began feeling his way. He was in a large room cluttered with all sorts of furniture and piles of objects, some of metal and some of cloth.

Any minute, he expected the trap door to reopen to void men and guns. His throwing the key had seemed like the smart expedient, but if this room turned out to be locked from the outside, it would not prove to have been so clever after all.

As he steered his course among the obstacles he at last found a wall and began feeling his way along it. He covered one wall, bumped his head against an unseen bronze statue, made a right angle, and continued some meters along the next wall before he came to a door. And what a door! A huge bronze affair, as wide as he could span with his arms, and, moreover, one of a pair.

The door was closed (as he found by fumbling) by a large bolt on the inside. He pushed the bolt, and then the door itself. The huge valves swung silently open.

Bulnes found himself facing a row of small Doric columns interconnected by a metal railing, and beyond that a larger row. Ahead, slightly to the right, the massive form of Athene Promachos towered against the stars, topped by the triple-crested helmet of the goddess. He now knew where he was—on the porch at the west or rear of the Parthenon. The room in which he had emerged from the tunnel system was the storage room occupying the rear third of the building. This room, Flin had explained, was the true "Parthenon," the temple as a whole being properly the New Hekatompedon.

Bulnes turned, pushed the great doors closed again, and hurried to the bronze rail and climbed over.

He trotted down the steps at the end of the Parthenon and sprinted for the Propylaia, dodging art works by starlight. He had almost reached his goal when from the forest of columns in front of him a deep voice with a Scythian accent spoke: "Who there?"

Damn the Scythians! Bulnes ducked behind a statue and paused, watching and listening. Boots stamped on the marble in front of him. He headed back the way he had come, crouching. Any minute now, the back doors of the Parthenon might fly open to disgorge more enemies.

Right in front of him, Bulnes recognized a statue to which Flin had called his attention when he had shown him the place. It was Myron's bronze Athene, a slender, girlish goddess more to Bulnes's taste than the beefy colossal Promachos by Pheidias. As Bulnes remembered his colleague's chatter, this statue was to be one of a pair. The other statue not yet mounted was to be that of the satyr Marsyas.

Marsyas's base was there even if the satyr himself was not. With the Scythian archer coming up behind him and the puppet-masters in the Parthenon in front, Bulnes adopted a desperate expedient. He shucked his chiton, wrapped it around the papyrus, and threw the bundle away.

Then he mounted the pedestal of the statue of Marsyas, naked, and struck a statuesque pose. It was too bad his skin was too dark to pass for marble and too light for bronze. But, in the starlight, perhaps nobody would notice.

The doors of the Parthenon opened, and a small group of men came out. By rolling his eyes Bulnes saw that they were dressed in chitons. They spread out purposefully. One passed not far from Bulnes, but behind him. It took all the will power Bulnes could summon not to turn his head.

The voice of the Scythian archer came again from the direction of the Propylaia. Somebody blew a whistle, and the men in the chitons ran back to the Parthenon. In a matter of seconds they were all inside, and the doors closed again.

This time the Scythian came on with determination, calling out: "Who there? Who you? I see you! Come out, you thief!"

Bulnes stood very still as the fellow clumped past, not ten meters away. The policeman continued on his way to the west end of the Parthenon. He sniffed around the porch, like a willing but none too intelligent watchdog, and then walked back toward the Propylaia. Bulnes cursed silently and waited a few minutes longer. Heat lightning flickered on the horizon.

When the Scythian failed to reappear, and the rear doors of the Parthenon stayed shut, Bulnes slipped down from his pedestal, donned his chemise, rolled up his battered papyrus, and set out for the north side of the Akropolis. Flin had said something about stairways down the mountainside at this point.

It took him an hour of solid, sweat-soaked searching to find the stairway he sought. It was hidden behind a screen of bushes and architectural froufrou so that none would have suspected its presence. The stair led down, not on the outside, but into a cleft where the whole north side of the Akropolis had come adrift from the main body of the rock. The stair sloped down through the crack between this colossal slab and the solid part of the crag.

Bulnes had to feel his way step by step through nearly total darkness. He should, he thought, be approaching those caves on the north side of the Akropolis that Flin had pointed out. He had to move, however, at such a snaillike pace that it took him nearly half an hour to cover a hundred meters.

The stair at last leveled out, its risers becoming shorter and shorter until he was shuffling along a path at the base of the cleft. After many minutes more of feeling his way, he got a glimmer of light from ahead: yellow lamplight, if he was any judge. There came a murmur of voices.

Now and then, the cleft came together so that he had to squeeze through the gap. The voices grew louder. Bulnes found himself standing at the back of a cave—no doubt one of those he had seen from below. It was actually a double cave, two caverns having a common mouth. The light and sound were coming from the other, mostly out of sight around the rocky bulkhead that divided them.

There was a stir of motion at the cave entrance. A man in a long chiton came around the bulkhead toward Bulnes. Bulnes shrank back into his tunnel.

The man came, not at Bulnes, but toward his left. Arriving at the cave wall, back where the rocks narrowed, the man pulled aside a curtain and squeezed into a hole in the rock. The curtain fell back into place, inconspicuous among the other offerings and objects ranged around the wall of the cave.

When the man did not reappear, Bulnes stole forward toward the cave entrance to where he could see the proceedings. The other cave contained an altar before which stood a priest. Something burned on the altar. On a ledge that ran along the cliff, level with the cave floor, stood a row of men—evidently the suppliants or worshipers.

The priest had his arms up in a gesture of blessing, intoning a prayer. When he had finished, he said, "You may ask, O man!"

The first man in line stretched his arms out, palms up, and called loudly: *"Otototoi, Theoi, Ge! Apollon! Apollon!"*

When he had repeated the exclamation three times, a hollow, inhuman voice resounded from the back of the cave, "I am here, O man. Speak!"

Bulnes nearly jumped out of his skin when the voice first sounded, though a second's reflection showed him what the true cause of it must be. The suppliant continued, "O Averter of Evil, tell me what I should do to make my wife conceive?"

"Let her eat three mustard-seeds while facing east on the night of the next full moon, at moonrise, and do thou pay ten drachmai to the priest of this shrine of Apollo. Next!"

The next man wanted to know if the trading voyage in which he had invested eight mnai would be successful, and so on. Bulnes grinned, realizing whither the other priest had been bound when he disappeared into the hole in the back of the cave.

This method of milking the Athenian public also gave Bulnes the germ of an idea. More than one man could play Apollo.

He waited until the last inquirer had received his reply, paid his scot, and departed; until the two priests had tidied up their caves, counted their money, put out their lamps, and departed. Then Bulnes came out of hiding and prowled along the ledge until he came to the north wing of the Propylaia, stole down the steps, and thence homeward. Poor Wiyem would have to go supperless; it would be impossible to buy food this late.

Bulnes staggered into the inn of Podokles, pacified the growling watchdog, and fell asleep almost before his head struck his pallet.

FIFTEEN

The sun was high when the flies and the noise of
Athens at work finally awoke Knut Bulnes. He
opened an eye. Then, at the realization that he was
late for his lecture, he leaped to his feet, feeling
light-headed from lack of food. He would not even
have time to feed poor Wiyem Flin if he did not
want to jeopardize the chances of his getting the
bail money from Kritias.

One thing about the Athenian way of life, there
was no tedious routine of washing and shaving
and hunting for a clean pair of socks in the morning. He already had on his chiton, and looked
around for his himation. Then he remembered
discarding it in the Theseion last night when in-
vading the tunnels.

Bulnes had picked up enough Athenian cul-
tural attitudes to know that he could not pass for a

philosopher without a cloak, and would therefore
have to procure one even if he went without
breakfast. He got the address of a weaver from
Podokles (there was no such thing as a tailor in
Athens) and half an hour later was hurrying toward the house of Kallaischros with another
two-by-four-meter rectangle of cloth swathing his
lanky figure.

Kritias said, "Where have you been? We have
waited half the morning. What sort of teacher are
you?"

Bulnes made his apologies, adding the lie that
he had had to feed his poor friend Philon, rotting
away in the Oikema.

"Speaking of which, my dear sirs," he continued, "I believe it was agreed yesterday that the
noble Kritias should put up the money to bail out
my colleague?"

Kritias looked blank. "I remember nought of the
sort. True, you mentioned some such matter, but
we explained that neither of us was in a position
to help you. Is that not so, Demokritos?"

"It is not! Indeed, Kritias, you definitely promised Bouleus the money. No, do not wink. As this
man has dealt justly with me, I intend to see him
dealt justly with by others."

Bulnes could have hugged Demokritos, except
that in Classical Greece such a gesture would be
misconstrued. Kritias, grumbling, went out and
presently came back with a bag that clinked.

"Hold out your hands," he said, and began
counting out silver coins, most of them massy de-
kadrachma as big around as an Imperial silver
kraun and a good deal heavier.

"Four hundred seventy, four hundred eighty, four hundred eighty-four, four hundred eighty-eight, four hundred eighty-nine, four hundred ninety, five hundred drachmai," he said. "By the Dog, have you not brought a bag?"

Bulnes stood with fingers spread, a great pile of coins filling his cupped hands and a lot more scattered on the ground at his feet. He had not before thought of the disadvantages of the lack of paper money and checks for large sums.

"I shall manage," he said. He laid the money down and did as he had seen Athenians do: pulled his belt tighter and stowed the silver inside the breast of his chiton, the belt retaining it from falling through. The total mass, weighing nearly five pounds, was cold against his midriff.

Three hours later, Bulnes and the Polemarchos came to the Oikema and found the jailer. The Polemarchos said, "Release the prisoner Philon. This man has gone bail for him."

The jailer led them around to the side of the building where Flin was confined. The prisoner glared silently at them as the jailer unlocked the fetter on his leg, then stood up, flicked an insect from his clothes, and followed them out of the cell.

The Polemarchos said, "I was going to schedule your trial for the seventeenth, but since your friend here says Euripides has promised to withdraw his complaint, I will put it off to the twenty-fifth. By then we should have heard him."

"Thanks you, dear sir," said Bulnes, and turned to Flin. "I suppose you're hungry enough to . . ."

"Hungry!" howled Flin. "Have you been trying to starve me to death? Here I've missed three meals, and the bugs ate me alive, and not a word from you! I see you've got a new himation. Been having a gay time chasing the women, I suppose?"

"Shut up," said Bulnes.

"What? What's that?"

"I said shut up! *Calle su!* Must I make it plainer?" Bulnes cocked a fist. "If you'll come along to the Agora like an adult, we'll buy some food for Podokles to cook, because I haven't had a bite in the last twenty-four hours either."

Flin subsided, muttering. As they walked through the marketplace, Bulnes told of his adventures. When he came to the place where Thalia, alias Melite, admitted him to the house of Euripides, Flin burst out, "How did she look? What did she say? Did she show any signs of knowing me?"

Bulnes went on with his story, censoring the part where the woman had made an obvious pass at him.

Flin said, "When can I see her again?"

"You can't, my dear comrade."

"What d'you mean, I can't? We can use that manuscript as an excuse for calling on Euripides, can't we?"

"I mean several things. For one, you've already got yourself in bad with them by your outburst at the play. For another, it was just luck that I happened to see her. These Athenians normally keep their women shut up like a lot of medieval hidalgos, as you well know. Sometimes I think it's a good idea, too. And for another, it's a fifteen-kilometer hike down to Peiraieus and back, which I don't care to face again soon."

"But—but—dash it all . . ."

"Take it easy. It would only upset you without accomplishing anything, as she wouldn't know you. We'd best leave the Euripideses alone while we figure out our next move."

Bulnes went on to tell of his nocturnal experiences in the tunnels and on the Akropolis.

". . . so I went home," he concluded, "and I should have got up earlier this morning except—what's the matter, my dear Wiyem?"

Flin's mouth was puckered up and tears ran down his plump cheeks. "I—I can't help it. You've destroyed my last hope that this could be the real thing," he blubbered. "Now I know it's a stage show. Never mind me—I'm just a useless old pedant. Sorry I flared up just now, old thing."

Bulnes was reminded of a puppy that, surprised in some misdemeanor, lies on its back and waves all four paws in an effort to propitiate its gods. You can't very well kick the beast no matter how angry you are. He said, "The silver plate in Diksen's head must be the reason the broadcast wave doesn't affect him."

Flin had recovered his composure. "What's this idea of yours?"

"If we could get a message to Perikles, telling him to appear at the Cave of Apollo, we might get into that priest hole back of the cave and interview him. If he were tipped off to the nature of this act that's going on, this historical pageant, he might do something about it."

"Would he believe you?" asked Flin.

"That's why we should pose as Apollo."

"Mm. The real Perikles was a skeptical sort of blighter. And what'd you mean by 'we'? You don't think I'll risk my neck on any such stunt, do you?"

"Yes, I do. If we can convince him that he and all the other pseudo-Greeks are being used as puppets in a game, maybe he'll dig into the tunnels and break up the show."

"That part's all right, but why must I be in on it? You're a venturesome sort of chap, but I'm no ruddy good at playing Red Indian, you know."

"The language, my dear fellow," said Bulnes with elaborate patience. "How impressed d'you think he'd be by an Apollo who talked broken Greek with a Spanish-English accent?"

"Well I'm not going," said Flin, tightening his lips.

"Why not?"

"If you must know, I'm terrified."

"*No es verdad?*" said Bulnes with an ominous tilt to his eyebrows. "I think you will. Unless you prefer to go back to the Oikema, while I return the bail money to Kritias . . ."

"*Oy!* You wouldn't!"

"Wouldn't I? Try me and see."

"Oh, damn and blast!" Flin stamped his foot. "Why do you always get the better of me? A dashed tyrant, that's what you are. A sneering, haughty, cold-blooded autocrat.

"Thank you, dear comrade. Let's finish up here. You'll have to write that letter for me."

"When were you thinking of staging this interview?"

"Tonight, if possible. I don't wish to give Perikles time to devise a trap for us."

Two hours later, much improved by a meal, Bulnes and Flin got to work upon their letter. Using the manuscript of Euripides as a guide to penmanship, Flin wrote:

Phoibos Apollon to Perikles Xanthippou of Cholargos, Strategos Dekatos Autos of the City of Athenai:

If you will present yourself alone at the Cave of Apollo tonight, the tenth of Elaphebolion, two hours after sunset, having taken measures to insure that our conversations shall not be interrupted, you shall hear matters of grave import to yourself and to the state.

Flin said, "I can't guarantee that'll fetch him. It looks like an attempt to get him alone for abduction or murder."

"Oh, he'll have friends or slaves within call. Now let's get Diksen and case the joint, as they say in America."

Diksen, once awakened, was full of enthusiasm for the scheme. He walked them along the base of the Akropolis, below the statues of the Tribal Heroes, and pointed out significant features.

"That split in the rock runs back to another cave—see that dark spot?—they call the Aglaurion after some dame in their cockeyed religion. There's two stairs going up from the bottom of the split to the top, one at the Aglaurion end and one in the middle. And see that path going up to the wall? Where the old guy is sitting with the goats?''

He pointed ahead to the eastern part of the north side of the hill. "There's a hole in the angle of the wall and another stair going up to the top. These stairs ain't really secret—I went through 'em all when my beat was up there—but the priests try to keep the common people out."

The next task was the delivery of the letter. They hiked over to the house of Perikles. Bulnes made friends with a little girl playing in the filth of the street and bribed her with a copper to deliver it. He and Flin watched from around the nearest corner until they saw the letter handed to the porter.

They ate early and went up to the Akropolis before sunset, wearing chitons only, when the main crowds were beginning to come down. They turned left as they issued from the Propylaia and walked to the enclosures along the north side. To Bulnes the area looked quite different by daylight, so that it took him some time to identify the route he had followed the night before.

When he finally found it, they waited until nobody seemed to be looking and hid among the shrubbery. It proved easy—too easy, Bulnes feared. After the sun had set, a couple of Scythians went by shooing the remaining visitors off the Akropolis. However, they made no effort to beat the bushes for lurkers.

With nothing to do, Bulnes found his mind wandering to Dagmar. Should he ask her to marry him on his return—assuming he ever returned to twenty-seventh-century London? After all, he was pushing forty. Yes, he resolved, he'd ask her at the first chance.

The evening hush came over the area. A pair of priests went by, talking in low tones about money.

"Follow me," said Bulnes. He led the way, crouching, to the head of the stair down into the cleft.

Although the sky overhead was still light, the cleft was so dark that Bulnes had to feel his way again. At the bottom of the stair, he led Flin along the rough mass of stones and earth that filled the bottom of the cleft, until they reached the Cave of Pan.

"Here we wait," said Bulnes.

"Dash it, I wish I had a cigarette. Why do you think of these wild schemes, Knut?"

"Mixed ancestry, no doubt. Keep your voice down."

As the light dimmed, footsteps sounded in the adjacent Cave of Apollo, and the voice of a priest, "No, my son, the god will not present himself tonight. Come back tomorrow with your questions." Then, as the footsteps of the inquirer receded along the ledge, the same voice spoke again, "It is plain robbery and oppression that Perikles should ask exclusive use of the shrine tonight. Why can he not take his turn like any other citizen? That is your so-called democracy!"

"Will the god give him a message?" said another voice.

"After he has cost us two or three mnai in fees? Not this embodiment of the god!"

"We might give him something short and am-

biguous, as they do at Delphi. You remember
when Kroisos, the Lydian king, asked whether he
should . . ."

"Ea! Since he has had so little consideration for
us, he can stand there all night without answer for
all of me. 'Message of importance to the state,'
forsooth!"

The conversation wandered off into the love
lives of the two priests. It was punctuated by a
sharp tapping which Bulnes identified as the im-
pact of a flint against a piece of steel or pyrites.
Presently there was the faint crackling of the altar
fire and the smell of incense.

At last there came more footsteps along the
ledge, and the priests' voices, "Rejoice, my dear
Perikles!"

"Rejoice," said a new voice.

"This is an honor. It has been years since you
visited our shrine. The Ruler of the Seasons will
be pleased."

"I daresay. But since the Bright One specifically
asked me to present myself alone, would you
gentlemen mind . . ."

Bulnes was sure he had heard that voice before.
It was a staccato voice, speaking in short phrases
and biting off the ends of its sentences with a
snap. Bulnes remarked, "That jerky voice doesn't
sound to me like a great orator."

"That's Perikles," whispered Flin. "He was
really a curt, taciturn sort of chap, and Aspasia
wrote his speeches."

"Come on." They crept toward the secret entrance to the priest hole. He thrust the curtain
aside and they slunk into the tunnel until they
reached the opening behind the altar.

The head priest was saying, ". . . but my dear, dear Perikles, it would be against all precedent. The Health-Giver would be offended if we absented ourselves . . ."

There was a crackle of papyrus and the voice of Perikles, "There you are. I know not what this means, but I intend to find out. Will you go, or must I call for help in removing you?"

"Oh, we go, we go. But say not that we failed to warn you."

"Not that way. This way. I do not care to be deceived by human voices issuing from holes in this rabbit warren."

Bulnes looked through the funnel-shaped hole into the Cave of Apollo. Beyond the altar stood the two priests, their backs more or less to Bulnes. Beyond them stood Perikles. All Bulnes could see through the smoke of the altar fire was a neatly trimmed gray beard and a himation. The priests went out and turned left along the ledge. Perikles came forward toward the altar. "Phoibos Apollon, if it indeed be you, I have come as you requested. Have you a message for me?"

"Go ahead," whispered Bulnes, pushing Flin into the place behind the speaking hole.

Flin said, "O Perikles, it is indeed the God of the Silver Bow. You and all your people have been subjected to a monstrous deception, and it is time this imposture were unmasked."

"How so, O god?"

"You are not Perikles Xanthippou, nor are the other Hellenes the persons they think they are. The true Perikles lived three thousand years ago. You are a man who has been seized by the world rulers, and by their science caused to believe that

you are indeed this ancient Perikles, and the other
Hellenes have been subjected to the same deception."

"Indeed?" Perikles took the news, Bulnes
thought, with unwonted calm.

"Just so. If you wish proof, order your people to
dig down into the floor of the Parthenon chamber
of the New Hekatompedon, and below the altar of
Theseus in the Theseion, to discover the tunnels which the servants of the world rulers use
for . . ."

Flin broke off and jerked back from the orifice.
Bulnes took a quick look through the hole, to see
the man called Perikles coming around the altar
and drawing a pistol from his draperies. In that
second the altar fire blazed up. By its light, Bulnes
recognized the face he had manipulated scores of
times in making up the dummy for the next issue
of *Trends*: Vasil Hohnsol-Romano, ninth of the
name, and Emperor of the Earth.

Bulnes tumbled back in his turn. As he did so,
the piercing crack of a shot smote his ears and
fragments of rock stung his face. Again and again
came the crack of the shot mingling with the crash
of the explosive bullet. A hit from one of those
little pellets would blow a man to pieces.

He crawled after Flin toward the curtained entrance and collided with him. "*Caray!* What the
hell?"

"He's coming around this way," quavered Flin.
"Look!"

"What?" Bulnes craned his neck backwards.
The shooting had stopped and the heavier dust
particles were settling. By the fugitive light of the

altar fire, through the now-enlarged orifice,
Bulnes observed that the explosions had broken
away a concealed door at the rear of the priest
hole.

Bulnes thought he heard footsteps in the Cave
of Pan from which they had come. Wherever it
led, the newly revealed door seemed to offer more
safety than a cave containing an armed and
homicidal emperor. Bulnes scurried back into the
hole. The explosions had smashed the bracing
that held the lock, so that a good heave opened the
door. Bulnes scooted through, Flin after him.

"Close it!" hissed Bulnes.

As the door closed, they were again plunged
into darkness. Not complete, however. As his
pupils dilated, Bulnes became aware of a row of
tiny spots of softly glowing light along the roof of
the tunnel in which they found themselves. These
were ordinary radioactive night lights. Gradually
his vision sharpened until he could dimly see the
floor and walls.

He proceeded, crouching, until the tunnel
ended in a T intersection. The new tunnel, at right
angles to the old, was somewhat higher and carried a mass of cables along its roof.

Bulnes turned left at hazard and followed the
lights of this tunnel. It dipped down and did a
couple of dog legs, then ended with a door that
reminded him of the pressure doors through
watertight bulkheads on large ships.

On the wall beside the door was a push button.
Below it was a legend, illuminated by a brighter
night light, which, in English, instructed the way-
farer to push the botton to summon a guard to

open the door and admit him to the tunnel system.

Bulnes said, "I don't think we'd better do that. Let's try the other direction."

They retraced their steps to the tunnel leading to the Cave of Apollo, but continued straight on instead of turning. Bulnes, puffing up the slope, said, "We know a couple of things now: Not only is Perikles really Vasil the Ninth, but he's an unconditioned man like us and like Diksen."

"How d'you know that?"

"Would he be shooting a pistol otherwise? Of course he doesn't believe in Apollo, and as soon as he heard your voice he guessed another unconditioned man was talking to him from hiding."

"Do you suppose he's putting on this whole Greek thing as a sort of grandiose charade to satisfy his vanity?"

Bulnes shrugged in the gloom. They had come to the end of the tunnel. There were no outlets except straight up. The cables overhead led up, and so did a ladder, into a dimly lit cavernousness above.

Bulnes craned his neck, peering up, then started to climb. He soon found himself squirming through a jungle of struts and crossbraces, lit by a whole constellation of night lights. Around him rose an irregular structure of dark greenish metal.

Flin said: "By Gad, Knut, I know where we are!"

"Where?"

"Inside Athene Promachos!"

"Really? Let's hope we don't give the dear lady indigestion. This reminds me of the Statue of Liberty in America. Where do those cables go? Wish I had a flashlight . . ."

Bulnes finally reached a point that he judged to be somewhere on a level with the solar plexus of the goddess. From there, looking up, he could see where the cables ended in a forest of metal antennas, something like radar antennas: clusters of rods and plates arranged in patterns.

"There they are," he said.

"There are what? Oh, those things." Flin fell silent. After puckering his mouth with thought for some seconds he said, "Of course I don't know a ruddy thing about electricity, Knut, but I thought radio and radar antenna had to be out in the open—that a lot of metal around them would smother the rays or whatever it is they send out."

"That's true on the electromagnetic spectrum, but not on the gravito-magnetic. You know those things the World Government scientists were playing with a couple of decades ago?"

"No."

"Well, I'm not a scientist myself, but the magazine has a tickler file on gravito-magnetics, and once every few years we try to find something out about it. There was a lot of activity, with prophecies of the wonderful things it would do for us, and then it dropped out of sight. As far as *Trends* knows, not a single scientist is interested in it any more."

"So you think they've been developing this secretly?"

"It looks that way."

"Why?" asked Flin.

"I'm just guessing, but I suspect it's what keeps all our pseudo-Greeks under control."

Flin looked speculatively at the cables. "If we could cut through those, we'd queer the whole pitch at once."

Bulnes shook his head. "Probably electrocute ourselves in the process, and they're armored, so it would take days even with a modern hacksaw. It would be more to the point to find the master switch that turns off the power. Let's see. There ought to be a door in the lady's skirts at street level. . . . Here we are. Get ready to slip out quietly . . ."

Presently Bulnes and Flin emerged from the colossus and hurried toward the northeast corner of the Akropolis, in search of the stairway that led to the base of the wall and the path down the hillside that Diksen had shown them that afternoon.

SIXTEEN

A sound awakened Knut Bulnes. As he opened his eyes the first thing he saw was a pair of Scythian trousers, surmounted by a Scythian jacket and, above that, the broad face of Roi Diksen.

"Hey, Mr. Bulnes, how'd it go off, huh? I was scared . . ."

"Ssst!" said Bulnes, indicating the other sleepers.

"Aw, those dopes don't understand English . . ."

"Shut up, O barbarian!" groaned one of Podokles's other guests. "I am fain to sleep."

"We'd better go out," said Bulnes, and shook Flin awake.

They wrapped their himations about them and issued into the street. The sky was pale in the east, though the sun had not yet risen. Bulnes shivered a little in the predawn cold.

Diksen said, "Now what the hell happened? I'm patrolling my beat in the Kerameikos, see, and hear a racket from the Akropolis, and this morning the boys is talking about how the big shot went to the Cave of Apollo and the god shot off a couple of thunderbolts to show he was the real McCoy. I was expecting maybe as how you guys had gotten plugged."

Bulnes told their story.

"The Emp!" exclaimed Diksen. "You know what? He's up to something, I bet."

"Your gift for understatement," said Bulnes, "is magnificent, my dear Roi."

"Oh, but that ain't all! Perikles passed out an order to begin arms inspection for the militia, a tribe at a time. So the whole Erechtheis tribe is gonna parade outside the Dipylon Gate this A.M., two hours after sunrise. He'd have made it earlier only there wouldn't be time to pass the word. Then tomorrow it's the turn of Aigeis."

"Can we watch?" asked Bulnes.

"I dunno why not. Looky, let me catch a little sleep, and I'll meet you out here two hours from now."

"But your lecture appointment!" said Flin.

"You, my dear friend," said Bulnes, "will take care of that."

"But really . . . I ought not to take it on impromptu . . ."

"*Carajo!* You helped me prepare the lecture, and you can have the fun of trying to remember the subjunctive aorist of 'to be' for a change."

"Oh, very well," grumbled Flin.

At the appointed time, Bulnes headed for the

Dipylon Gate. As he slopped through the dirt he became aware of great numbers of Athenians making in the same direction, armed for battle. Every one of them carried a round shield, of wood and leather with a thin bronze facing, with a big A painted upon it. Each bore a light six-foot pike and wore a crested helmet. Most also wore a cuirass of bronze or of studded leather, a kilt of studded leather straps, and bronze greaves. As the throng funneled toward the gate, remarks flew:

"Oi! Stop pushing!" "Hurry up, Andokides, or I will prick your . . ." "What is the meaning of . . ." ". . . so I said, give me a hetaira like Theodote . . ." "Where have you been, O Strymon?" ". . . I am sure he stole it from the people, but you know juries . . ." "Eia, come along . . ." "Maybe there will be war after all . . ." ". . . I told him, if you think you can cheat Hegias and get away with . . ." ". . . my tooth has been driving me . . ."

Outside the Dipylon Gate, men were falling into ranks. Scythians were directing spectators to one end of the formation, and Bulnes let himself be shooed along with the rest. From there he could look down the front rank—a somewhat serpentine and irregular one, but brave in bronze and iron. In front of the militiamen stood a small clump of men among whom Bulnes could make out the handsomely bearded figure of Perikles-Vasil with a Corinthian helmet pushed back on his head so that his face showed.

It took the hoplites an interminable time to get squared away, for this force seemed weak in officer organization, and every soldier argued all the time at the top of his lungs. At last they shook down into hundred-man companies. Perikles called, "Attention! Men of the tribe of Erechtheis, stand upright. We will pass among you to see that all weapons and defenses are in good condition."

He began moving slowly toward where Bulnes stood. Bulnes experienced a moment of panic before he remembered that, happily, Perikles had not gotten a good look at his face the night before.

Perikles, followed by the other men of his group, arrived at the hither end of the front rank of the hoplitai. He stood there for a long time, looking down the line and sometimes exchanging a word with the other officials: "Behold those potbellies! We must needs institute some special exercise to reduce them . . ."

His manner was that of one who has all the time in the world; or, Bulnes thought, one who was deliberately killing time.

"Let us go, Perikles," said one of the officials at last. "We cannot keep them standing in the sun all morning."

Slowly, perhaps reluctantly, Perikles moved down the line, stopping for a long close look at each militiaman. Bulnes heard him say to the second man in the line, "That cracked old shield will never save you from the spears of the enemy. See that you have a new one at the next muster . . ."

"Hey, Mr. Bulnes!" came a stage whisper, and there stood Diksen. "Sorry, but I guess I kinda overslept. How's it going?"

"At this rate, the inspection will take all day."

They watched as the figures of Perikles and his colleagues dwindled with distance and their voices became inaudible.

Then, suddenly, it happened.

Every soldier gave a jerk, a start, or a shudder. Spears toppled right and left as their holders let go of them to turn and stare in amaze at those around them. There was a clatter of shields; men felt their beards, patted their cuirasses. From the armed mass came a rising murmur. Bulnes, listening, caught sentences in modern Greek, and some in other languages.

"*Pu ime?*"

"*Christe! Ti ine afto?*"

"What's this thing on my head? A cuspidor?"

"I don't get it. I'm punching the cash register in my restaurant, and next minute I'm out here with a manhole cover on my arm . . ."

"What am I, a Papal Guard?"

A few, taken by panic, ran off across the plain. The rest babbled questions, louder and louder until the din became deafening. Perikles stepped back from the line and shouted, "All those who understand me, step this way!"

The confusion, however, became more chaotic with each second. A number of men did step toward Perikles, but not, apparently, because they understood his Attic. Instead, they menaced him with their spears and yelled demands for an explanation.

Now the crowd around Bulnes reacted, too. There were murmurs of: "Madness!" "Witchcraft!" "The gods have smitten us!" "They speak in strange tongues!" "Flee for your lives!"

Then, when it looked as though anything might happen, the hoplitai started again and stared around wildly as they had done at the beginning. They began wandering back to their places in line and picking up their discarded equipment, asking each other, "What happened?" "What happened?"

"Get back in formation!" cried Perikles. "We will carry on the inspection."

And, his companions still following him, he walked back to where he had been at the moment of the outburst and continued down the line. Now, however, he walked rapidly, giving each man scarcely a glance. In a few minutes it was all over. The citizens, dismissed, were streaming back to the city, still asking questions of each other and of passers-by.

"Well," said Diksen, "what do you think of that?"

Bulnes frowned. "It looks to me as though those antennas inside Athene Promachos must control each of these Greeks individually. Each is on a different wave length, as it were. I suppose his people underground have a card file of all the Greeks, and he told them to check off all the male citizens of the tribe of Erechtheis, and then at a predetermined time to throw the switches that controlled them. He must have hoped to catch one or more unconditioned men by watching to see who didn't start capering and asking where he was."

"I getcha. Don't seem to me as how that'd work, though. Too many people all yacking away at once."

"Right. Don't be surprised if you hear the inspections of the other tribes have been called off."

They picked up Flin at the house of Kallaischros and wended their way to the Agora to buy their lunch. Flin, eating an omelet wrapped in leaves, listened to the account. "He's determined to uncover the unconditioned men at all costs," he commented. "We'd jolly well better do something."

Diksen said, "I wonder they don't just run through their card files to see who Philon and Bouleus are, and when they find there ain't no such people, they'd know you guys is it."

Bulnes said, "Remember, they've probably got two or three million people in Greece. That's too many to keep close track of without modern police methods, and you couldn't apply such methods without giving the game away."

"Another thing," said Flin. "The fact that the Greeks had no real surnames would make it harder to keep track of them. You might have several hundred men named Leon, and one of them might sometimes speak of himself as Leon son-of-Lykos, another time as Leon of Phaleron, and still another as Leon the Short or Leon the Stonecutter. You can see the difficulty of keeping an eye on each of your Leons. There might be scores of Bouleuses, and how are they to tell there's an extra one and expose him except by turning off the ruddy machine?

"By the way," continued Flin, "Kritias says a couple of his friends want to join our course."

"Splendid, my dear fellow," said Bulnes. "We shall be successful in spite of ourselves."

"There's one catch, though. The crowd's getting too large for the house of Kallaischros. We shall have to move out."

"The Agora's too noisy for my taste," said

Bulnes, glancing over to where Sokrates was arguing: ". . . but my dear Antiphon, if everyone
takes the view that morality is simply a matter of
who can think up the cleverest arguments to support his interests, what becomes of public virtue?
How long will such a state endure?"

Bulnes added, "How about one of the gym-
nasia?"

"It would have to be the Kynosarges," said Flin,
"since the others don't admit noncitizens. But
what shall we do about the Emp? I have no doubt
they can locate us eventually." Flin turned to
Diksen. "Any chance of fomenting an insurrec-
tion among your fellow-gendarmes?"

"Huh?"

"He means," said Bulnes, "could you stir up the
rest of the Scythians to revolt?"

"Dunno. Doubt it. The Scythian cops got a good
deal. They can keep women on the side and when
they get too old for work, the commissioners
turn 'em loose. Usually they've grafted enough by
that time to set 'emselves up in business or go
back home." He yawned prodigiously. " 'Scuse
me, fellas, I gotta get back to barracks to catch
some sleep. You forget I'm up all night."

He left.

Flin said, "Speaking of this and that, hadn't we
better see if Euripides has sent his letter to the
Polemarchos yet?"

Bulnes shrugged. "Considering that Euripides
is the original absent-minded professor, we shall
probably have to remind him a couple of times
before he'll do it."

To his surprise, however, Bulnes learned that

the letter had been delivered to the Polemarchos that very morning.

"Kephisophon must have remembered to remind him," said Bulnes. "My dear sir, is my friend now a free man again?"

"Yes," said the magistrate. "If you will wait, I will send a slave to the treasury to fetch your bail money. Have you two found a patron yet?"

"No," said Bulnes. "We approached the good Sokrates, but he—uh—could not see his way clear."

"That subversive agitator, always unsettling our young men by questioning the wisdom of our ancestors! It is just as well for you that he refused. However, be advised to find a patron soon, as you will be entered upon the tax rolls in any case and you might as well have the legal standing of a registered metoikos."

The money came, and Bulnes and Flin departed to return it to Kritias. Bulnes said, "I'm sorry we weren't there when the slave arrived. We could have sent Euripides' manuscript back by him. In this world it always takes ten times as much fumbling around to accomplish a simple thing like that as in our own."

Flin nodded. "I miss jolly old London myself, fogs and all."

SEVENTEEN

Late that afternoon, they were sitting in the inn of Podokles and working up the next few days' lectures, when Dromon the slave came in.

"Sirs," he said, "a message from my master Sokrates. Perikles is giving a dinner and symposium tonight at his house, whither he has invited all the philosophers of Athens. He asked my master to round up any he, Perikles, might be unacquainted with, wherefore Sokrates sent me to seek you men of Tartessos."

Bulnes exchanged looks with Flin, asking, "What's this?"

Flin said, "That's out of character. The real Perikles wasn't a very sociable chap—seldom entertained and seldom appeared in public except on state business. D'you think he'll try to smoke us out the way he did the militia this morning?"

"It wouldn't surprise me. But, being fore-
warned, we sould be able to cope with it."

"You mean when the others go off their rails,
we do likewise?"

"Precisely."

"Dash it all, it seems like taking a frightful risk.
Why don't you go and leave me?"

"What did you say?" said Bulnes, glowering.

"But—I mean—you could say I had a head-
ache . . ."

"It'd be an even worse risk to refuse. You're
going. Dromon, what do we do now?"

"Follow me. My master will lead you to the
house of Perikles."

Sokrates greeted them cordially at the Agora.
He evidently could not stay angry long with anybody who looked like a promising antagonist in
an argument. Bulnes had tactfully worked the
philosopher around to the subject of becoming
their *prostates* when they arrived at the house of
Perikles.

The Strategos greeted them with grave cor-
diality inside the door. Bulnes took a sharp look
at the Athenian statesman. There was no doubt
that the man was the Emperor. Meanwhile,
Perikles-Vasil was looking just as keenly at
Bulnes. He said, in the manner of one making
polite conversation, "It is interesting to meet one
of the fabled Tartessians. Are you of the race of the
Keltoi, said to inhabit the westernmost parts of
Europe?"

"No, Perikles."

Flin spoke up. "We are the autochthones of

Iberia, and cultivated the arts and sciences there centuries before the coming of the barbarous Kelts."

"Your name is Philon, my dear sir?" said Perikles.

As Perikles turned his head, Bulnes noticed the remarkable length of his skull, which projected backward to a conspicuous degree. Had he made a mistake? Vasil IX had no such bulge.

Within the andronitis, Bulnes found all the philosophers he had already met—Protagoras, Demokritos, Anaxagoras, and Meton—and several others he did not know. Nobody bothered with introductions; all were too busy with converse. Meton, for instance, was explaining his proposed calendar reform to somebody and railing at the stupidity of the masses who insisted on using an obsolete and irrational system of time reckoning from sheer force of habit. Flin said, "That one with the squint is Diogenes."

"The fellow who lived in a barrel?"

"No, you're thinking of the Cynic philosopher, who wouldn't be born yet. This is a scientist. And that's Prodikos, the one with the theories about the nature of myth, just back from Italy . . ."

Prodikos was telling Protagoras: ". . . and I stopped at Thourioi and saw Herodotos."

"How is the old fellow?"

"Still amazingly vigorous—working on a history of Assyria, and hopes to visit Athens next year . . ."

Anaxagoras was upbraiding young Demokritos, who tried to hide behind pillar: ". . . so you come all the way from Abdera to study

philosophy, and never think to seek out poor
old Anaxagoras? What a heedless generation it
is . . ." Demokritos was stammering apologies.

"Dinner, gentlemen," said Perikles. The crowd
padded barefoot into the andron.

Bulnes murmured to Flin, "I could surely use a
double Martini!"

He found himself paired with Antiphon the
sophist, a youngish man about the age of Demokritos. Flin reclined on the next couch. Bulnes,
watching him, had to admit that the little schoolteacher adapted himself to the Athenian style of
eating more adroitly than he himself did. A slave
appeared with a towel and a basin and began to
wash Bulnes's feet.

Antiphon looked at Bulnes with a sneer and
said, "So Perikles, far from giving me the place of
honor, puts me with a foreigner! That shows his
true opinion of the better sort of people. No of-
fense meant to you, my good man—after all you
cannot help where you were born."

The interior of the house of Perikles was little
different from the other houses Bulnes had seen;
less sumptuous than that of Kallaischros, but
perhaps a little neater and roomier than Meton's.
The Athenians' genius certainly did not express
itself in interior decoration of private houses. A
young woman who, Bulnes thought, would have
been better for a good wash, sat on a stool and
tweetled away mournfully on a thing like a
clarinet. The monotonous little tune reminded
Bulnes of a Gregorian chant.

Antiphon, his mouth full of endives, said,
"Man of Tartessos, judge not all Athenian ban-

quets by this one. Our Long-Pate Zeus is too serious-minded for party giving. You should attend one of those of our livelier spirits, like the young Alkibiades . . ."

As the fare was spare and simple, the actual eating did not take long. The clatter of argument among the philosophers almost drowned out the music of the *aulos*.

Perikles cleared his throat, and said, "Gentlemen, ere we begin the symposium, may I bring Aspasia in to listen?"

When nobody objected, Perikles spoke to a slave, who went out. Antiphon said to Bulnes behind his hand, "That is one advantage of a concubine. You cannot decently bring a legal wife into such a gathering. And the funny thing is that Perikles cannot marry her because of a law he caused to be passed years ago, forbidding unions of citizens with foreigners . . ."

Aspasia swept in—a tall, handsome woman of about Bulnes's own age. "Gentlemen!" she said. "It is most kind of you to permit me . . ." She sat on a chair instead of reclining.

Antiphon said, "Wait till they get under way. She will tie some of their fine theories into knots. Woman though she be, the Milesian has a shrewd and penetrating wit."

A pair of slaves lugged in three big bowls and set them on the floor in the middle of the horseshoe in which the couches were arranged, while others carried out the teetery little tables on which the food had been served. Bulnes, watching this process, felt his chiton twitched from behind. There stood a slave holding out a fistful of straws.

Taken aback, Bulnes glanced around, observing that several others had each drawn one. He drew one also.

Perikles presently announced, "The short straw has been drawn by the good Archelaos, who is hereby appointed Master of Ceremonies. Do you take command, O Archelaos."

The graybeard across the horseshoe from Bulnes rose and commanded, "Mix the wine in the proportion of two to one."

Bulnes thanked his stars that the lot had not fallen upon him. As the slaves poured the contents of one wine jar and two water jars into the big bowls, Antiphon said, "We should have Kratinos the comedy writer in charge. He would mix one to one and then drink half a krater himself."

Archelaos scooped some of the diluted wine out of one of the bowls with a ladle, said something about "the Olympian gods," and poured the wine on the floor. He poured two other libations: "To the Heroes," and "To Zeus the Savior," and sprinkled incense on the altar.

Bulnes realized that those about him were singing to the tune of the clarinet. He listened, trying to catch the words:

> "In mighty flagons hither bring
> The deep-red blood of many a vine
> That we may largely quaff and sing
> The praises of the god of wine."

"Now," said Archelaos, "the subject for this evening will be the origin of the universe."

Antiphon emitted a groan, echoed by several others.

"I knew it!" moaned the sophist. "One might as well die under Spartan spears as expire of boredom. The Anaxagoras will go on all night about his theory of primal seeds. But perhaps you foreigners like this sort of thing?"

Archelaos frowned at Antiphon and continued, "I shall first call upon our young friend from Abdera. Speak, O Demokritos!"

Demokritos turned a bright red above his fuzzy beard. "I—uh—er—I do not really know—ah—uh—I am unworthy—uh—I pray, do not . . ."

"Come, come, have either cape or cloak," said Archelaos.

Demokritos smiled nervously. "Well—ah—Leukippos taught me that first there were atoms and the void, and —uh— after all I am nobody compared to the distinguished men here—but as these atoms fell through the void, we think—ah—the differences in their weights would cause some to fall faster than others, thus setting up eddies—uh—er—and these eddies condensed into solid particles . . ."

While Demokritos stumbled along, in obvious torment, Bulnes shot a glance at Perikles. The latter was looking at Demokritos with a faint and not unsympathetic smile, then down again to a piece of papyrus in his hand. Could that, Bulnes wondered, contain a list of those present, so that Perikles-Vasil could check them against the card files of his pseudo-Greeks?

"I say, Knut! Watch Meton!" It was Flin, whispering from the next couch.

Bulnes saw that the astronomer was undergoing the same process that he had observed on the drill field that morning. He swung his feet down from his couch and sat up, staring wildly, and exclaiming in modern Greek: "Where am I? What is all this? Are you people pretending to be ancient Greeks, or what?"

Demokritos broke off, staring like the rest. Meton started to rise, then looked down as his sole garment, an unpinned chiton thrown carelessly around his body, began to fall to the floor. Meton clutched wildly.

Antiphon said, "By Herakles, that is the same seizure that is said to have smitten the soldiers on the drill field this morning! Is Athens undergoing an epidemic of universal madness?"

"Damn it," cried Meton, "say something! Doesn't anybody understand me?"

Then Meton looked around a little foolishly, and resumed his couch. Anaxagoras cried, "What ails you, O Meton?"

"Why?" said Meton in Classical Attic, "What do you mean? I had a slight feeling of dizziness just now and found myself standing, but now I feel perfectly normal."

"Do you not remember speaking gibberish?" asked Sokrates.

"Not at all. What is all this? Are you men jesting?"

Bulnes leaned toward Flin and murmured in English, "Perikles must have made arrangements to turn off the radiations for his guests one at a time, in a predetermined order."

"What shall we do? If they don't all rave at once, how shall we know when to rave?"

"We shan't. But then if he orders his men to check the list, they'll find out that neither of us is listed in the card file."

"Oh-oh!" said Flin. "I knew we were ruddy fools to come. Let's get jolly well out of here!"

"Not yet. A few more like that will break up the party anyway, and we don't want to look conspicuous."

Aspasia said, "Go on, dear Demokritos. You were doing splendidly!"

The interruption, however, had so unstrung that shy young man that he was unable to get anything out but er's and ah's. At last Archelaos said, "We will come back to you, O Demokritos. Meanwhile the Sokrates, having been declared by the oracle to be the wisest man in Athens, will perhaps favor us with a few words on this profound subject?"

"It is notorious that I am the stupidest man in Athens," said Sokrates, "or I should not find it necessary to ask so many questions. As for the origin of the universe, I think that a question of no great importance—since, whatever caused it, it happened long ago, and the problems of leading a good and virtuous life are more pressing.

"However, since you wish it, I will tell you a story I have heard from my Pythagorean friends. They argue thus: As all corporeal things are generated, so must the cosmos have been generated, which implies a generator or maker. This maker, for lack of more definite knowledge, we call 'the gods.' Thus, you see, they avoid the crass materialism of our scientific colleagues. And this maker must have constructed the universe of the four elements theretofore existing—earth, air, fire, and water, as Empedokles teaches—leaving over no single particle or potency of any one of these elements. And the maker intended that the universe should be a living creature, perfect and whole . . ."

Bulnes, watching Archelaos, saw him stiffen, look wonderingly at Sokrates, and cry in modern Greek, "What's all this? I'm Eleftherios Protopapadakis, and I had just dismissed my class . . ."

This time the uproar drowned the words of both Sokrates and Archelaos. Then the latter sprawled back on his couch as if nothing had happened.

"Let us continue," said Perikles. "Whatever these strange seizures be, they do not appear to last long or to have ill effects. If you will resume your talk, Sokrates?"

Bulnes, watching, saw Perikles scrutinize the sheet of papyrus in his hand and make a motion that looked like checking a name off a list. The party had now become so disorganized that it took five minutes for Archelaos and Perikles to quiet the guests. Sokrates resumed:

". . . so the gods, in their first attempt at creating intelligent creatures, constructed androgynous bodies each with four arms and four legs. But, these proving awkward, the gods in their kindness caused these creatures to fall asleep, and while they slept the gods split each of them lengthwise into two parts, one part being a human male and one a human female, and thus the two sexes came into existence . . ."

There was more, about the mathematical proportions the gods had used in designing the universe, the supersouls of the earth and the stars, and the motions of the planets—all very involved and couched in jaw-breaking compound terms.

Antiphon muttered, "He may not be the stupidest man in Athens, but he can certainly be the biggest bore when he tries."

Bulnes shook his head in assent.

Antiphon persisted, "There is no doubt he is a just man, but by his very excess of virtue he commits an injustice."

"How so?"

"He insists on lecturing all comers gratis, comparing honest teachers like the Protagoras and myself to harlots because we ask a fair return for our labor. And in this way he discredits us and encourages our pupils to beat down our modest fees by threatening to go hear Sokrates instead. Which is depriving us unjustly of our livelihood."

As the sophist chuckled over his own cleverness, Bulnes, finding the ideas expressed by Sokrates not only difficult to grasp but so scientifically obsolete as to be not worth grasping, turned his attention again to Perikles.

The statesman was glancing at his papyrus and then up. Bulnes said to Flin, "Look—he's waiting for the next one."

"Looks to me as if he were wondering why the next one hasn't gone off. Notice how the blighter stares at Aspasia!"

It was true. The glances of Perikles at his consort became longer and more intense until Aspasia herself became conscious of them and showed signs of unease. She even leaned toward Perikles and whispered a question.

Sokrates droned on: ". . . and thus the gods made bone: They sifted earth until it was pure and smooth, kneaded it, and moistened it with marrow, and by alternately dipping it in fire and water, so wrought upon it that it was no longer soluble in either. Then on a lathe they turned out the spherical bone that forms the skull . . ."

"Knut!" said Flin in an undertone. "Don't you think Perikles expects Aspasia to be the next to go?"

Bulnes nodded. "I wonder if she's an uncon—"

At that instant a scream cut through the monologue of Sokrates. Aspasia had leaped up from her chair and was backing away from Perikles, who had also risen.

"So," said Perikles, "you're the spy from Lenz, eh?"

"No—no . . ."

"Then how is it that you speak English?" Perikles advanced menacingly. Gone was his quietly cordial, elder-statesman manner. The guests stared open-mouthed.

Aspasia retreated toward the door into the court. As she neared it she spun round in a whirl of draperies and ran. Perikles drew a dagger from his chiton and ran after her.

Bulnes saw nothing suitable for a weapon save the ladle with which the wine in the kraters had been mixed. He leaped from his couch, snatched it up, and ran after Perikles.

Aspasia vanished through the door, Perikles after her, and Bulnes after Perikles. At the middle of the andronitis Aspasia detoured around the altar. The slight check enabled Perikles to catch up with her and drive the dagger into her back.

Almost simultaneously Bulnes, with a leap of his long legs, reached Perikles and struck him with the ladle on the back of the head. There was a crunching sound and Perikles fell forward over the body of his mistress.

"Ea! What is this?" cried Protagoras from the doorway. "What a horror! A sight for Aischylos to describe! I am leaving. Boy, my shoes and cloak! Hurry!"

All the other guests began shouting for their slaves and their gear. They streamed past the group in the court, some carrying their sandals and himatia without bothering to don them, and rushed out through the front door, crying:

"The furies must have done this!" "A curse has fallen upon Athens!" "I was not even here this evening!"

Bulnes then heard exclamations among Perikles' own servants: "The master stabbed the mistress, and then the foreign gentleman broke the master's head . . ."

In a few seconds, they, too, were running out. Bulnes knelt and pulled Perikles off the body of Aspasia. Both were alive. Bulnes examined the head of Perikles and discovered that the projecting back of the head was a false structure of plaster, covered with a wig, which he had broken with the ladle. Perikles was merely stunned; Aspasia was in worse case, blood dyeing her chiton.

Bulnes looked up. Flin and Sokrates stood beside him, but otherwise the house seemed empty.

Sokrates said, "Such a devoted couple, too! And now all their fair-weather friends have run, lest one should be accused of having a hand in this business."

"How about you?" said Bulnes.

"I care not. How are they? Dead?"

Bulnes gave his diagnosis.

Sokrates said, "The boy, their son. Some older friend must prepare him, and I seem to be the one chosen by the gods for the purpose. I shall be back presently."

He disappeared into the back of the house. The woman who had passed as Aspasia opened her eyes, stirred, and coughed up a little bloody froth. She said, "Get—message—to Lenz."

"Yes?" said Bulnes.

"Tell him—Vasil—suspects." She coughed. "If he—wants to seize—the machine—to use on the world—do it now."

"Why should Lenz wish to do that?" asked Bulnes.

"Power. Tell him—hurry."

"And what's the Emperor up to?"

"To make—people happy. He thinks—they were happiest—in time of Perikles. If he can make all the world—live that way—he . . ." She went into a spasm of coughing.

"Why is he running this dress rehearsal?"

"He thinks—he can avoid—the mistakes—of the original Perikles. Bring back the Golden Age."

Flin said, "For God's sake, let's do something for her . . ."

Bulnes waved him to silence. "Why," he asked Aspasia, "are you helping Lenz?"

"I work—for him. He pays well—and Vasil's—a fool."

"Where can we hide until we can carry this message?"

"Try Kleon. Enemy of Perikles."

"How accurate is this re-creation of Athens? Has Vasil any special means of viewing the past?"

"No. His experts—read books and studied relics—like other people. Tell—Lenz . . ."

Her voice trailed off and her eyes closed. Though her pulse still beat, she seemed to have lost consciousness. Bulnes said, "I don't know that there's much we can do for her, Wiyem. No modern physicians or medicine, and she'll probably die shortly."

"How about him?"

"Merely a slight concussion."

"By Jove, that puts us in a fix! We can't very well carry her through the streets—the moving would probably kill her anyway—and if we leave her here, he'll come to and finish her off."

Bulnes shrugged. "Unless I did *him* in now."

"Gad, not that!"

"You're probably right, but for the wrong reason. No use bumping Vasil when Lenz would turn the conditioning machine on the world. And as everybody knows we were the last to leave the house, he'll be able to figure out that we're un-conditioned, too. So it won't do for him to find us here when he comes to."

Bulnes felt Aspasia's pulse again. It still beat feebly. He felt guilty about her, but he could see no other course.

"Sokrates is still around," he said. "He can do about as much as we can, which is damned little. Come on—we're going to Kleon's."

EIGHTEEN

Kleon's porter said, "I will call the master."

After a wait, the door opened. A big voice rumbled, "Come in, you two. What is this great news you have for me?"

The torchlight showed a man as tall as Knut Bulnes, stout and potbellied, with a great mop of curly hair, a scanty beard, a snub nose, and small close-set eyes. The man, Bulnes judged, must be some years younger than himself. As he looked more closely, he realized that the man was holding a short Greek sword.

"It is this, O Kleon . . ." began Flin, but subsided when Bulnes trod on his toes.

Bulnes, sizing up the man, said, "Excuse the intrusion at such an unseemly hour, good Kleon, but the news is indeed momentous, especially for you. First, know that we are but two traveling philosophers from far Tartessos, who . . ."

"Get on with it," said Kleon. "Is the Perikles dead, or what?"

"Not exactly."

"How mean you, not exactly?"

"The news is almost that important. But hear me. We, having through no fault of our own fallen foul of Perikles, seek sanctuary—for, as unregistered foreigners, we have little protection. In return for our news we look to you to provide it."

Kleon thought, then said, "If you do not mind living with my slaves and if your news be as important as you say, very well. Now let us have it."

"Perikles has just murdered Aspasia."

"*What?* Impossible!"

"True nevertheless. And before all the philosophers of Athens, so you can easily confirm my story."

"Tell me quickly! No, first come in and shut that door. We would not have all the world from Caria to Carthage hear."

Bulnes told the tale of the symposium, omitting his own knowledge of the causes of the outbreaks of seeming dementia and the true identity of Perikles.

"By the twelve postures of Kyrene!" shouted Kleon, slapping his thigh. "This is indeed the world's wonder!"

He began pacing back and forth in the andronitis.

"This will finish that compromiser, that seducer of the people! Now they shall come into their own. No more appeasement of Sparta. No more pampering the subject cities. Athens shall

be mistress of an empire like that of the Great
King. Every Athenian citizen a king! And I will
show the rotten rich, too. Kleon the Tanner they
call me, the perfumed weaklings, because I make
my living by honest slave-driving instead of letting some slimy metic manage my affairs. Well, I
will tan their hides so they shall long remember it.
I will grind them underfoot as I will grind our
rebellious and ungrateful allies. But how to top-
ple old Long-Pate from his pedestal? Ha?"

He glared at Bulnes, teeth bared in a mirthless
grin.

Bulnes said, "Not being too familiar with Athenian law, I do not know, but could not he be
arrested for murder?"

"Who should arrest him? Action against a murderer must be brought before the King by the next
of kin of the victim. Aspasia was a Milesian with
no relatives in Athens, save her son by Perikles,
who is only a boy."

Flin squeaked, "Could not her patron take action?"

"Yes, save that her patron is this same Perikles.
Would you have him accuse himself?"

"Well then, could not the Polemarchos, as legal
guardian of all metics, do it?"

"You raise a nice point of law which, so far as I
know, has never been settled. It might work—we
Athenians have no patience with legal subtleties
that defeat justice. First, however, I think I had
better go to the Tholos and take up the matter with
the President of the Council. The Presidency will
call a special assembly tomorrow to remove
Perikles from office for unfit conduct. You two

wait here until I return! Boy, my shoes and himation."

As the front door closed behind Kleon's bulky
form, Flin said, "That's a dangerous man, Knut."

"So I gathered. What did the real one do?"

"I believe when he got power he persuaded the
Assembly to have the whole population of some
city massacred or enslaved because they wouldn't
join the Delian League—no, that was another
time. He did carry such a motion, but then somebody else persuaded 'em to cancel the order—in
the nick of time."

"We shall have to watch ourselves. You know,
comrade, I can't help feeling I've seen Kleon
somewhere before, too."

"I wonder who he could be in everyday life?"

"I don't know. It's just a feeling. At least some
things are becoming clearer."

"Such as?" said Flin.

"Vasil's general pattern. What happened to the
original Athens at this point?"

"The Peloponnesian War broke out, you
know."

"Yes, but in detail?"

"Oh, good heavens, it was a long and complicated war . . ."

"The Athenians lost?"

"In the long run, yes."

"And that war, you say, ruined Classical
Greece?"

"More or less," said Flin.

"Why did Athens lose?"

"As I recall, several reasons. One was that
Perikles died of a plague at the outset and the

Assembly went off its rails without him to guide it. They elected people like Kleon and Alkibiades to be their leaders, and did irresponsible things—like executing all their generals because, when they won a naval battle, they failed to recover all the bodies of their dead."

"What a crazy thing to do! Why?"

"Oh, they were superstitious about burial. Next day, when the generals were dead, they changed their minds and executed the men who'd made the original motion."

"Temperamental, no?"

"Also, they'd been exploiting the subject states of their empire until the latter hated them and were glad to break away."

"But I thought they were the great ancient democracy?"

"They were. You're used to modern history, in which aristocrats and authoritarians are the imperialists. In Athens the common people were imperialists and militarists, while the rich and the aristocrats were for peace and moderation."

"Why was that?"

"Because the rich were mostly landowners whose property would be occupied by the enemy in a Spartan war, while the *polloi* got their living from overseas trade and hence favored expansion of the empire."

"I begin to see," said Bulnes. "Vasil thinks Periklean Athens was a high point in civilization. If Perikles—that is, himself in an earlier incarnation—hadn't made some errors of judgment and hadn't died at a critical time, it would have gone on getting better and better. So, he thinks, why not re-create it by means of the conditioning machine his scientists have developed, and run the picture over with himself playing Perikles? This time, however, he'll profit by the experience of the real Perikles. He'll stave off the war with Sparta. He'll conciliate the allies, offering them union on equal terms as a modern statesman would do. Then, when he's re-established the ideal civilization on a stable basis, he'll build a superconditioner and put the entire world under its influence."

"How could he, since the Emperor has no political power?"

"How could he get this far? Lenz let him, either to keep him out of his hair or, more likely, because Lenz hopes to use the conditioner himself on the world. If Vasil weren't fundamentally a fool, as Aspasia said, he'd have seen that. What a way to keep everybody under control! And you could justify it by saying that they were all as happy as possible, even if they weren't in their right minds."

Flin said, "I see their point of view, though they'd have had to modify their scheme for different climates. You couldn't live through a Russian winter in a chiton and himation."

"Oh, it's a cracked idea of course. There's nothing about keeping the slaves—a third of the population—happy, and I suspect these high points in history are inherently unstable."

"Why?"

"Some professor has a theory that they come up only when a society is changing from a basis of status and tradition to one of contract and reason, and the same forces that make the society flower also make it go to seed."

"I say!" said Flin. "We ought to let Diksen know."

"He'll find out about the murder, if that's what you mean. Everybody in Athens will hear of it, even without newspapers."

"I meant where we are."

"We shall have to see what Kleon does first."

Kleon returned to his house some time later, grinning.

"I fixed them!" he roared. "The Perikleans among the Prytaneis tried to delay things, but I showed them. The trumpeters have already gone out to sound a special assembly for tomorrow morning. It is too bad that you two cannot witness my triumph. We were going to attack Perikles through some of his friends, but this is quicker. To your pallets, and do not try to leave. I may need you as witnesses if there is a trial."

NINETEEN

An hour before dawn, the blast of the trumpets awoke Knut Bulnes. As he listened, the notes died away, to be repeated from a greater distance, and then a still greater until they were barely audible. That, he thought, would be the trumpeters sent out the previous night to the neighboring towns of Attika: Peiraieus, Acharnai, and the rest.

When he and Flin crawled out of their smelly little cubicle, Bulnes found Kleon in the court, and pacing restlessly.

"I go," said the Tanner. "You two may eat what you like, get drunk, bed a slave—it is all the same to me. But leave not until I permit you."

He nodded toward his front door, where a couple of stalwart slaves with clubs stood prepared to enforce the order.

Flin said, "My dear Kleon, we have an appointment at the house of Kallaischros, to lecture Kritias and Demokritos."

"Who is Demokritos?"

"A young philosopher from Abdera in Thrace."

"Well, Kritias as a citizen will be in the assembly with his father—rotten reactionaries, the whole lot—and Demokritos as a foreigner does not matter."

"At least," said Flin, "send a message telling them we shall be unable to come."

"I cannot be bothered," shouted Kleon. "The fate of Athens hangs in the balance, and you trouble me with your petty appointments. *Iai* for the people of Athens!"

Kleon strode out with his slaves. Flin said, "Last night this seemed like a nice, safe refuge from Perikles; today it seems more like a trap."

Bulnes smiled thinly. "My thought precisely. I suppose we shall have to spend the morning on vocabulary drill while the excitement goes on at the Assembly."

Bulnes was halfway through the list of proparoxy-tone adjectives when the porter accosted him: "Sir, there is a Scythian archer at the door, one Pardokas, to see you. Shall I admit him?"

"By all means," said Bulnes. Then, as Diksen came in, "My dear Roi, how the devil did you find us?"

Diksen grinned. "You can't hide nothing from slaves, see? The Gricks talk like we wasn't even there, and of course we pick things up and trade 'em back and forth. What's the dope on the big shot sticking a shiv in his beasel?"

Bulnes told him.

"Jeepers, what do you know?" said Diksen. "Things is hotting up. I s'pose this means I gotta stay up all day." He yawned. "Gotta get over to the Pnyx for this special assembly. Don't take no wooden nickels!"

The morning dragged on. Toward noon Bulnes heard Kleon's bellow outside. As the Tanner came in he took a crack at the porter with his walking stick, roaring; "That will teach you to open promptly when I call! Ho there, you Tartessians!"

"Yes?" said Bulnes. "Did something go wrong?"

"It might have been worse. I had presented my case, and all was going well, when the followers of the Perikles made an uproar, yelling like Illyrians till the President declared he felt an earthquake and adjourned the session because the gods were displeased. Gods!" He spat. "I had no time to bring up my main point—that for a long time Perikles has been receiving mysterious visitors who slip away from his house and disappear. One of my men followed one of these to the Theseion, where the fellow vanished into thin air. Spartan spies without doubt, arranging the betrayal of Athens. However, we shall continue tomorrow. Where is my lunch? Quick, scum, before I beat you to a jelly!"

The slaves scurried to obey. As Kleon waited there came another knock. In came a man.

"What is it, Hermippos?" said Kleon.

The man replied, "The squill-head is rallying his friends on the Akropolis with arms! We shall have a tyranny by nightfall, if nought hinder."

"What stops us?" said Kleon. "We have arms, too."

"But the constitution . . ."

"I will give the people a better one when I have ground their enemies into the mire. Sosias, my arms! Hermippos, run, tell Glykon and Diopithes and Drakontides and our other friends to arm themselves and rouse their friends . . . Here, I had better give you a list. Where is that worthless secretary of mine? Tell them to mark a big delta on their shields, with charcoal, delta for demos. Let them assemble on the path leading up to the Propylaia within the hour."

His slaves helped him into his greaves and cuirass.

Flin said, "This isn't in character either. The original Perikles was a good democrat who was once legally deposed without attempting violence."

"This isn't the original Perikles," said Bulnes. "He only thinks he is. My dear Kleon, you have no more reason to keep us here. Let us go, if you will be so kind, and if you wish us later, you can get in touch with us at the inn of Podokles."

"Go to the crows, for all I care! Now let me think. We want Hagnon and Simmias and Lakratidas . . ."

Bulnes and Flin slipped out and headed for the Akropolis. Bulnes said, "If Kleon wins . . ."

"That dreadful man?"

"Precisely, comrade. That'll end the experiment, no matter what happens to Vasil. Somebody'll turn off the conditioner . . ."

"Not necessarily. Lenz might simply take it

over, whether Vasil's killed or not, as the first step in his own program."

"Then I suppose it's up to us to turn it off."

"How?" said Flin

"*No se.* If we had some explosives, or even a power saw . . ."

"Could we loop a rope around the neck of the statue and pull it over?"

"Doubt it. You'd need half the rope in the Arsenal of Philon and a couple of hundred men . . . *Dion!*" Bulnes clapped a hand to his head. "I know who Kleon is!"

"Who?"

"The long-lost Prince Serj, Vasil's brother! I knew I'd seen those pig's eyes somewhere."

Flin said, "How can that be? There's not that much difference between their ages."

"There's about fifteen years, in actual fact, and I think Vasil used makeup to look older. Just another of his queer ideas, to dispose of his brother by conditioning him to play the part of one of Perikles's enemies."

As they neared the Akropolis, Bulnes became aware of an occasional armed man making his way in the same direction. When they got within sight of the saddle between the Akropolis and the Areopagos, he saw several clumps of such men standing around the path that zigzagged up to the Propylaia, and a continuous trickle of more men was arriving. Most of those in the groups were holding shield and spear in one hand to have the other free for forensic gestures. As they approached, the sound of universal argumentation came to Bulne's ears like the cackle of a colossal barnyard. From the upper end of the path, where it wound among dedicatory tripods and statues, men continued on up into the pillared recesses of the Propylaia.

Flin said, "At least, at this stage, the Athenians were still a fighting race."

They paused to watch at a safe distance, along with many other unarmed or undecided Athenians. As the armed men became more numerous, they colaesced into two sets, one of the partisans of Kleon (identified by the triangle on their shields) and the other those of Perikles. The two sets shouted arguments, threats, and insults at each other.

Somebody among the Perikleans (who straggled up toward the Propylaia, leaving the Kleonians on the lower slopes) noticed the letter *delta* on the shields of the Kleonians. He went among the Perikleans drawing a big letter *pi* on their shields.

Kleon puffed up the slope at last, towering over his partisans like a liner among tugs. Bulnes could hear his bull's voice, but not make out the words.

"Let's move a little closer," he suggested to Flin.

"Really, old chap, isn't this close enough?"

"Nuts! Come on!"

Bulnes and Flin climbed higher up the saddle on the Areopagos side, where they had a good view. Kleon, pointing off to the northeast, cried, "Athenians, look upon the statues of the famous Tyrannicydes! Will you endure that another tyranny be riveted about your necks? It is time we had another heroic Harmodios, another Aristogeiton . . .''

The stream of Perikleans up the path had abated. Only a few straggled up now. Kleon roared, ''On which side strive these two coming up the path? Perikleans? Slay them! *Elleleleu!*''

There was a rush of hoplites and a clash of spear points on bronze. Then one Periklean was down with men jabbing at him, while the other, throwing away spear and shield as he ran, bounded down the path faster than his more heavily burdened pursuers could follow.

''Come back up here!'' yelled Kleon. ''Do not let yourselves be scattered!''

''Look that way,'' said Flin, pointing.

Below, somebody had organized a group of Perikleans and was marching them rapidly eastward along the north foot of the Akropolis. The afternoon sun gleamed on their arms. Kleon must have seen them too, for he told off a group of his men and ordered them, ''Hurry to the back stairs of the Akropolis and block it lest any more partisans of the satyr king go up that way!''

He waddled about, pushing men into position and haranguing everyone within earshot.

Bulnes said, ''They seem to take all day to get organized. At this rate, it'll be dark before they get around to fighting.''

''He's probably trying to make political arrangements before joining battle,'' said Flin. ''See those chaps coming up? There's the Polemarchos, and there's the King, and the rest are the other Archons. Kleon's a clever lad—wants the law on his side.''

Bulnes and Flin sat down, watching, while interminable conferences took place, with endless wagging of hands and heads and messengers came and went. In particular, messengers ran up the path into the Propylaia and back down to Kleon.

At length Kleon came to a decision. He began marshalling his forces. "The squill-head," he roared, "says he will treat with us up on the Akropolis, on the east porch of the Propylaia. Form a column of fours. Hold yourselves ready—straggle not. It may be a trap."

"Vasil is up to something," said Bulnes. "Let's go with them."

That, however, proved easier said than done. Under Kleon's direction, his men crowded up the path to the Propylaia so closely packed that there was no room for a mere spectator. Presently the column up ahead halted and began to bunch up.

"Spread out into the Propylaia!" yelled Kleon. "Make way—I am coming up. What do you two want?" he exclaimed, turning on Bulnes and Flin, trying to ride his wake up the crowded path.

"My dear Kleon," said Bulnes, "I know more about the plans and methods of Perikles than you can imagine. If you will kindly let us come up with you we may be of unexpected help."

"What do you expect for your help, eh?"

"Merely to see right triumph."

"Huh. Well, come along."

They pushed their way up to the Propylaia. There the press lessened somewhat, because the men had spread out among the pillars and along the steps of the great gateway.

At the east side of the Propylaia, where the steps reached the level of the Akropolis, Kleon's men ranked solidly among the columns. Looking between the plumes of the helmets, Bulnes saw why: A few paces away stood a counterrank of Perikleans, shields lined up and spears poised at shoulder height.

Kleon pushed through his own men into the open space between the two armies. "O Perikles," he shouted. "Come forth!"

"I am here," said Perikles, who had climbed up on the great bronze chariot behind the front rank of his own men. He wore his Corinthian helmet pushed back to show the Olympian calm of his regular features. Behind towered Athene Promachos.

"What means this attempt at tyranny, you murderer, you traitor, you tool of the rich, you creature of the Spartans?"

"No tyranny," said the brisk voice of Perikles, "but an effort to forestall an act by the Athenians which they might regret later. I have a message from the goddess Athene herself."

"Do you expect us to believe that you, a notorious atheist, would be entrusted with a divine message?"

"No. The goddess herself shall speak to you."

"Ha-ha. I suppose you will dress a tall woman in armor and pass her off as Athene, as did the other tyrant?"

"Not at all. Pallas Athene herself shall speak, right now." Perikles waved an arm towards the colossus. "Speak, O goddess!"

Bulnes almost jumped out of his skin when a

tremendous voice thundered forth from the statue of Athene Promachos:

"Men of Athens! Athene speaks to you. Know that the Perikles is no tyrant, nor yet a traitor or murderer, but my best-beloved foster-son. Trust him, follow him, support him in every way, and he will insure glory, peace, and prosperity for you and for your descendants, and honorable burial for you all. Turn against him, and nothing awaits you but defeat, poverty, and destruction. Those of you who have impulsively taken up arms against him, return to your homes and store your arms against the day when Athens shall lead all Hellas against the threatening hordes of encircling barbarians. Obey the laws, preserve the peace, join Perikles in making Athens a beacon-light for the world."

There was a moment of silence when the great voice stopped, broken by a squeal from Flin, "By Gad, a public-address system!"

Then came a clatter of arms as Kleon's men poured down the path from the Propylaia toward the city.

TWENTY

Bulnes, followed by Flin, plunged into the mob and caught the politician's military mantle as Kleon trotted down the steps of the Propylaia with the rest of the rout.

"What now?" said Kleon, turning a fat face gray with terror.

"It is a trick!" said Bulnes.

"How? That was no mortal voice—not even Stentor . . ."

"It is still a trick. Perikles has a machine for enlarging the voice, hidden in that statue. I can prove it, and I can destroy the machine. Rally your men before they all melt away."

"Rally!" bawled Kleon. "It is a trick! I can prove it! No goddess, but a bit of Thessalian witchcraft! It is a trick! To me, me men!" He turned to Bulnes. "You had better be right. If this be a trick on *your* part, it will be your last. Hagnon!

233

Diopithes! This way! Catch those runagates. It is a trick of the same sort Peisistratos played with the woman Phye."

He rushed about, catching a man here and a man there, shaking them, pushing them, and by sheer strength of personality rounding up nearly half his original force.

"And now?" said Kleon.

"Make sure you have the Propylaia blocked," said Bulnes, "so the Perikleans cannot come down. Then fetch me a lot of straw—say a few dozen beds—and a couple of jars of oil."

"What are you going to do?" whispered Flin.

"A good hot fire will melt the gravito-magnetic connections in the statue."

"What say you?" said Kleon.

"Never mind—get me that straw and oil, and a torch."

Kleon gave the orders that sent a score of men running down the hill into the city.

Bulnes said, "Make a speech or something to keep your men occupied until they get back."

"O Kleon!" called a man with a *pi* on his shield. "Perikles wishes to know when you will obey the commands of the goddess."

"Tell him to give us time. This is too serious a matter to be decided without discussion." Kleon addressed his own men: "Men of Athens, you know that Athene, most virtuous of deities, would not employ a notorious murderer and traitor as her messenger to mortals. What you have heard is certainly very impressive, but let us not be fooled as were our great-grandparents by Peisistratos of infamous memory a century ago. I have reason to believe that the voice you heard was a trick . . ."

He went on and on until the men he had sent out began to trickle back up the hill with their arms full of pallets.

"Kindly give me a few men to help, good Kleon," said Bulnes.

Under Bulnes's direction, they dragged their burdens to the Caves of Apollo and Pan. He led them into the Cave of Pan, into the passage to the priest-hole, at the sight of which some whistled. They went on into the tunnel leading back from that recess to the main subterranean tunnel system. Bulnes turned right at the intersection, climbed the slope, and presently stood under the interior bracing of the big statue.

He said to Flin, puffing beside him, "Wish I could knock off the lady's head to improve the draft. Do you see those things up inside the statue that look like women's hair ornaments? That is where your 'divine voice' came from. Pour some oil on the pallets and stuff them up inside the statue as far as you can."

When the oil-soaked pallets were all pushed into place, Bulnes himself thrust the torch as the nearest. The straw caught fire with a *floom*. They trotted out of the tunnel with thick smoke billowing behind them.

Back at the Propylaia, Bulnes said to Kleon, "You may go back up above again. Soon, Perikles' divine voice will be stilled for good."

"Out of my way," said Kleon, and stamped up the marble steps.

At the porch he halted. The Periklean forces had come forward a little way with the retreat of the Kleonians, but most were still massed around the chariot on which Perikles stood. Beyond the chariot, little curls of black smoke issued from the Promachos.

"O Perikles!" roared Kleon. "Look behind you! So much for your pretended goddess! If it was not a trick, let Athene speak again!"

Perikles looked around, uttered an exclamation, dropped off the chariot, and hurried over to the statue. He fumbled among her brazen skirts and opened the same little door Bulnes had come out of on the previous occasion. Then he leaped back as a mass of bright yellow flame roared out, preventing him from closing the door again. The improved draft stimulated the fire; its roar became plainly audible and the volume of smoke increased.

Perikles strode purposefully toward Kleon and Bulnes. "So that is what you have been up to! Well, if the play is to end, at least you shall not live to succeed me, you self-seeking rabble-rouser!"

He whipped a pistol out from under his cloak, took careful aim at Kleon (who stared uncomprehendingly) and fired.

The crack of the firearm mingled with the explosion of the bullet. Bulnes felt warm wetness spatter him and looked around in time to see Kleon, his head gone, fall backward.

"The Tartessian!" said Perikles in English. "Another spy for Lenz, eh?"

Perikles swung his pistol up; the Emperor's finger tightened on the trigger.

From behind Bulnes came a flat unmusical snap, followed by the thump of an arrow striking a human target. Perikles staggered back and fired one wild shot. Then came the twang of a second bowshot. With two arrows in his chest, Perikles-Vasil, too, fell back upon the flagstones.

"Didn't get here none too soon, did I?" said Roi Diksen. "Hey, look at Flin—the guy's fainted!"

At that instant the same strange agitation began to creep over the crowd of armed men that Bulnes had seen on the drillfield and again at the house of Perikles. Men dropped their spears and shields and turned in wonderment and alarm to ask each other in modern Greek who and where they were.

Bulnes stepped forward to where lay Vasil Hohnsol-Romano, Emperor of the Earth, and picked up the pistol. The Emperor looked up and said faintly, "Fools! I'd have made you a heaven on earth. The mob never knows what's—good for . . ." His head lolled.

Diksen said, "Hey, Mr. Bulnes, the gimmick must be off!"

Bulnes gestured toward the statue of Athene Promachos. The fire was beginning to burn itself out, though the statue still glowed redly in spots. He said, "That's our doing."

"Yeah? Then we're the only folks here knows what the score is. You better get up and tell 'em."

"I suppose so." Bulnes wearily hoisted himself onto the bronze chariot and spoke in stumbling modern Greek: "Gentlemen! If you will kindly listen, I shall tell you what's happened . . ."

An hour later he had finished his explanation, answered questions, and organized the nearest Greeks into an impromptu government of Athens: some to go down into the city and repeat his explanation to the bewildered people there, others to police the town until it could reorganize itself, others to accompany Bulnes into the tunnels. Diksen he made police chief, despite the latter's wail, "But I don't *want* no job here! I wanna get back to good old Yonkers! If I ever leave Kaplen's Hardware Store again, you can fry my guts in olive oil . . ."

Flin, revived, said, "I'm going to find Thalia!"

"Wait, my dear comrade," said Bulnes. "I have a task . . ."

"Oh, find somebody else! I haven't got a minute to spare!"

Bulnes watched him go, his anger subsiding into contempt. Then Flin's departure suggested something to Bulnes.

He led his men back to the Cave of Apollo, into the tunnel from the priest-hole. At the door opening into the main tunnels this time he pushed the bell button.

After a while, the door opened, disclosing a surprised-looking man in khaki trousers and shirt. Bulnes said, "Out of the way, my dear sir. The Emp's dead, and the broadcasting machine is wrecked. The show's over."

The man went for a pistol. Bulnes whipped up the Emperor's gun and fired, *crack!* When Bulnes could see again after the flash of the explosion, the man was dead on the floor.

Bulnes picked up the man's pistol, handed it to the nearest Greek, and led his men down the slope to the entrance beneath the Theseion. The man at the desk looked up open-mouthed as Bulnes thrust his pistol into his face and said, "Give me the key to the machine-gun rack, quickly, if you please."

Bulnes unlocked the rack and passed out the guns. In fifteen minutes he and his men had a hundred-odd employees of the project rounded up. All the switches had been pulled, including that which controlled the force walls surrounding Greece.

Bulnes told the Greeks, "Take them out and chain them up in the Oikema until we decide what to do with them. Here, you, my good man, where is there an outside telephone?"

When he found the phone, he dialed long distance, then England, then Trafalgar 9-0672.

"Are you there?" he said. "Is this *Trends Magazine*? Good. Put me through to Mr. Ritçi, please. Robert? Knut Bulnes speaking. I have a story for you. Put the recorder on . . ."

When he had given his editor-in-chief an account of the Periklean Project and his part in the recent events, he rang off and dialed Dagmar Mekrei's apartment.

"Why Knut darling!" she exclaimed when he had identified himself. "What on earth happened to you? You disappeared off the face of the earth last month . . ."

"You'll read all about it in tomorrow's papers, darling. I'm in Athens . . ."

"But you can't be! That's reserved territory!"

"Not any more, *mariposa*. Travel should be re-established in a few days."

"Then you'll be coming back to London?"

"Not quite yet. Ritçi was so pleased with the story I gave him that he told me to take as long as I liked. Now it happens that my little ship is at the bottom of the harbor . . ."

"Oh, how dreadful!"

". . . and it'll take weeks to raise her, since there's no modern salvage apparatus here. I thought you might like to fly down here as soon as the airlines are running again, stay here sight-seeing while I get the ship up, and sail back to England with me."

"Oh—Knut . . ."

"Yes?"

"I'm dreadfully sorry but—I'm married."

"You *what*?"

"Married. Remember Kaal Beiker? He's been asking me a long time, and when you disappeared—well . . ."

"When was this?"

"Four days ago. He moved in with me, and I expect him home from work any time now."

Bulnes gulped, feeling the blood rush to his face, then leave it. "Well—uh—thanks for telling me. I hope—I hope— Oh, hell! Good-bye, Dagmar."

An hour later Bulnes arrived, in dungarees and yachting cap, in front of the house of Euripides in the Peiraieus. He parked the motor scooter and then knocked on the door.

Euripides himself opened it. When Bulnes explained who he was, Euripides said, "Come in, come in, *o Kirie* Bulnes."

"*Efcharisto*," said Bulnes, complying.

"I'm really Kostis Vutiras," continued the long-beard, "formerly a reporter for the *Athenian Herald*. Your friend Flin is here. He has been telling me that for seven or eight years I've been living the life of Euripides, the ancient poet. I should find it hard to believe, except for this. . ."

He tugged the beard and led the way in.

"It is a little embarrassing," he continued in a lower voice. "I have a wife somewhere, too, and God knows what she's up to."

Flin sat on an eating couch with Thalia, who greeted Bulnes without any sign of remembering his previous visit. He said, "Here are your modern clothes, my dear Wiyem. The gods save me from riding a motor scooter over these roads again!"

Flin said, "Thanks. It'll be jolly having pockets once more."

Thalia asked, "Have you been in touch with London yet, Knut?"

"Yes. I phoned the story in and spoke to Dagmar."

"How is dear Dagmar after all these years?"

"She's somebody else's dear Dagmar now. She married that fellow Beiker a few days ago."

Thalia said, "Oh, Knut, I'm sorry!"

Flin, after a futile effort to control his features, burst into a guffaw.

"You find it amusing?" said Bulnes ominously.

"I'm s-sorry, Knut, really. But you go round all these years saying you won't be tied down by marriage, and no ruddy woman is worth it, and all that rot. Then, when you get stood up, you put on a face a meter long."

"It serves him right," said Thalia, "the way he kept the poor girl dangling so long. No wonder . . ."

Flin, who had been going through his clothes, brought out a radio no bigger than a cigarette case. He snapped it on. Presently it hummed and gave forth music.

"Where'd you get that?" asked Bulnes.

"Had it all the time. Didn't work inside the force field."

The radio said: "We interrupt this program to bring another special bulletin. News of the un-masking of the late Emperor's Periklean Project has reached the World Parliament in New York and has caused tremendous excitement. A number of Populist supporters of Prime Minister Rudolf Lenz have deserted him and gone over to the Diffusionists. It now appears certain that the government will fall, and that the twelve-year strong-arm rule of the Lenz Ministry is at an end. The coronation of fourteen-year-old Crown Prince Seril will take place . . ."

Flin said, "Wonder what they'll do with all these magnificent reproductions of ancient build-ings? Tear 'em down and set up the authentic ruins again? I should think they could sal-vage . . ."

Something gurgled; Euripides-Vutiras was pouring wine.

Bulnes said, "At least we can now drink our wine straight without being thought barbarians."

"What are your immediate plans, Knut?" asked Flin.

"To raise my boat. I don't suppose you'd be interested . . ."

"Oh, no! We're rushing back to England as soon as there's transportation. Why don't you ask Dik-sen to go with you? He's a handy young chap, even if no intellectual."

"Not a bad idea," sighed Bulnes, feeling old and unloved.

Thalia said, "Cheer up, my old Knut. If you

have changed your mind about women and are persuing honorable intentions . . . Wiyem, are there of my young cousins still unmarried?"

Flin pondered. "There's Ero, the one with the blue eyes."

"Splendid! I will arrange everything . . ."

Bulnes said, "Excuse me! I shall be glad to meet the young lady, but beyond that I prefer to do my own arranging. I know you of old, my dear Thalia. Hereafter I will do as I like, eat what I like, and not what some megalomaniac emperor thinks I ought . . ."

"Indeed?" said Vutiras. "Has it occurred to you that, even in your so-called normal, modern, twenty-seventh-century world, you may be merely somebody's puppet, as Mrs. Flin and I were in this one—only you haven't been clever enough to penetrate backstage?"

Bulnes and Flin exchanged an appalled glance. The latter burst out, "Oh, what a perfectly beastly idea!"

POUL ANDERSON

48923	**The Long Way Home**	$1.95
51904	**The Man Who Counts**	$1.95
57451	**The Night Face**	$1.95
65954	**The Peregrine**	$1.95
69770	**Question and Answer**	$1.50
91706	**World Without Stars**	$1.50
91056	**The Worlds of Poul Anderson**	$1.95
	THE SAGA OF DOMINIC FLANDRY	
20724	**Ensign Flandry**	$1.95
24071	**Flandry of Terra**	$1.95

Available wherever paperbacks are sold or use this coupon.

Ace Science Fiction, Book Mailing Service,
Box 690, Rockville Centre, N.Y. 11571

Please send me titles checked above.

I enclose $ . . . . Add 50¢ handling fee per copy.

Name . . . .

Address . . . .

City . . . . State . . . . Zip . . . .

Ursula K. Le Guin

10704	**City of Illusion**	$1.95
47805	**Left Hand of Darkness**	$1.95
66956	**Planet of Exile**	$1.95
73294	**Rocannon's World**	$1.95

Available wherever paperbacks are sold or use this coupon.

Ace Science Fiction, Book Mailing Service,
Box 690, Rockville Centre, N.Y. 11571

Please send me titles checked above.

I enclose $ . . . . Add 50¢ handling fee per copy.

Name . . . .

Address . . . .

City . . . . State . . . . Zip . . . .

ANDRE NORTON

89705	**Witch World**	$1.95
87875	**Web of the Witch World**	$1.95
80805	**Three Against the Witch World**	$1.95
87323	**Warlock of the Witch World**	$1.95
77555	**Sorceress of the Witch World**	$1.95
94254	**Year of the Unicorn**	$1.95
82356	**Trey of Swords**	$1.95
95490	**Zarsthor's Bane** (Illustrated)	$1.95

EDGAR RICE BURROUGHS

$1.95 each

THE CASPAK SERIES

47025	**The Land That Time Forgot**
65947	**The People That Time Forgot**
64485	**Out of Time's Abyss**

VENUS SERIES

66506	**Pirates of Venus**
49506	**Lost on Venus**
09204	**Carson of Venus**
21565	**Escape on Venus**
90193	**The Wizard of Venus & Pirate Blood**

INNER WORLD NOVELS

03326	**At the Earth's Core**
65855	**Pellucidar**
79796	**Tanar of Pellucidar**
79855	**Tarzan at the Earth's Core**
04636	**Back to the Stone Age**
47000	**Land of Terror**
75135	**Savage Pellucidar**

Available wherever paperbacks are sold or use this coupon.

Ace Science Fiction, Book Mailing Service,
Box 690, Rockville Centre, N.Y. 11571

Please send me titles checked above.

I enclose $ . . . . Add 50¢ handling fee per copy.

Name . . . .

Address . . . .

City . . . . State . . . . Zip . . . .

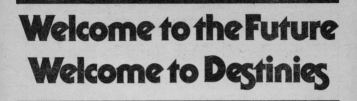
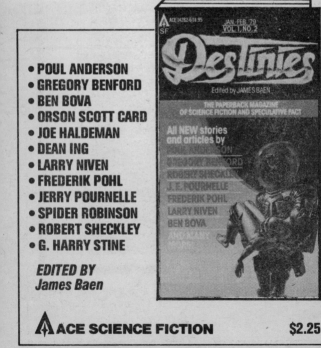